MOUNT VERITY

THERESE BOHMAN

Translated from the Swedish by Marlaine Delargy

Other Press | New York

Originally published in Swedish as *Sanningsberget* by Norstedts,
Stockholm, Sweden, in 2024.

The cost of this translation was supported by a subsidy from the
Swedish Arts Council, gratefully acknowledged.

SWEDISH
ARTSCOUNCIL

Title-page and part-opening illustration by Rawpixel.com
and Shutterstock.com

Production editor: Yvonne E. Cárdenas
Text designer: Patrice Sheridan
This book was set in Bembo Book by
Alpha Design & Composition of Pittsfield, NH

1 3 5 7 9 10 8 6 4 2

Printed in the United States of America on acid-free paper. For information write to Other Press LLC, 267 Fifth Avenue, 6th Floor, New York, NY 10016.
Or visit our Web site: www.otherpress.com

Library of Congress Cataloging-in-Publication Data
Names: Bohman, Therese, 1978- author | Delargy, Marlaine translator
Title: Mount Verity / Therese Bohman ; translated from the Swedish by
Marlaine Delargy.
Other titles: Sanningsberget. English
Description: New York : Other Press, 2026.
Identifiers: LCCN 2025033941 (print) | LCCN 2025033942 (ebook) |
ISBN 9781635425666 paperback | ISBN 9781635425673 ebook
Subjects: LCGFT: Bildungsromans | Novels | Fiction
Classification: LCC PT9877.12.O48 S2613 2026 (print) |
LCC PT9877.12.O48 (ebook)
LC record available at https://lccn.loc.gov/2025033941
LC ebook record available at https://lccn.loc.gov/2025033942

PRAISE FOR **ANDROMEDA**

"A confident, erudite novel, comfortable with developing at its own pace...Deeply provocative in its quiet contemplation."

—*Kirkus Reviews*

"A beautifully written book about a publishing company undergoing massive changes, a questionable and yet somehow aching relationship between an intern and her boss, nostalgia, the feeling of being left behind, and the ideals we cling to when everything is falling apart around us...a breath of fresh air in the literary world." —*Booklist*

"*Andromeda* is the best kind of company—a book I kept longing to return to, full of ideas and emotion."

—Julia May Jonas, author of *Vladimir*

PRAISE FOR **THE OTHER WOMAN**

"Equally erotic and shrewd, the latest from Bohman (*Drowned*) reads like a confession, or diary...The author's prose is breathtaking, oscillating between her narrator's tumultuous feelings toward her lover and the narrator's curiosity—and occasional disdain—for the world around her...An elegant, rich take on an age-old narrative." —*Publishers Weekly* (starred review)

"*The Other Woman* hooks the reader with a captivating voice and a dramatic spin on a story we've all heard before...This captivating, character-driven tell-all provides the reader with a unique insight . . . And [Bohman's] bashfully charming leading lady keeps you hooked until the very last page."

—*New York Daily News*

"A mesmerizing page-turner." —*New York Journal of Books*

PRAISE FOR **DROWNED**

"A slim novel with a taut narrative line and a sense of impending disaster . . . A tale of identity and tense personal relationships, one that as a film property would have appealed to Hitchcock or De Palma." —*Kirkus Reviews* (starred review)

"The seasonal and structural changes are deliberately understated and carry emotional weight into the climax, which Bohman deftly makes both foregone and suspenseful, leaving the reader wondering if everyone was doomed from the start."

—*Publishers Weekly*

"[Bohman] writes with simplicity and restraint, and each detail adds to the slowly building tension . . . This is an artful psychological thriller, and utterly riveting, as it delves into the dark side of lust, sex, and obsession." —*Herald Sun* (Australia)

MOUNT VERITY

ALSO BY THERESE BOHMAN

Andromeda

Eventide

The Other Woman

Drowned

FOR NELLY

No one finds me,
I find no one.

—CARL JONAS LOVE ALMQVIST

The highest is the most comprehensible,
the next, the most indispensable.

—NOVALIS

PROLOGUE

On Easter Saturday 1989 I recorded almost the whole of the Top 20. I had been given a cassette player for Christmas, and even though I had been interested in music before, my interest increased when I was suddenly able to record the chart for myself. That winter I spent Saturday afternoons in front of the cassette player: I recorded, recorded over a track, recorded again. It felt sophisticated, because I thought that what I was doing wasn't something my contemporaries did until they went to high school. Knowing which songs were in the chart made me feel grown-up.

There was plenty of drama in the spring of 1989. Debbie Gibson's "Lost in Your Eyes" had been at number one for three Saturdays in a row, but was knocked off the top spot by Paula Abdul's "Straight Up," which went straight in at number one. Or "*Straight up* to the top," as the radio personality Kaj Kindvall said. Genius.

On this particular Saturday I had to leave with just under half the chart still to go, because it was time for our Easter lunch. I rewound the tape back to the beginning of side B when Mom called me down, then I pressed Record and left the machine to its own devices.

I liked Easter, because it was peaceful and undemanding. Unlike Christmas and Midsummer, we celebrated at home without any visiting relatives, and without doing anything special. Four long days when everyone was free; Mom and Dad would be busy in the garden while I lay in my room reading, listening to music, and eating my Easter candy. I might go out on my bike at twilight, or watch a movie with Erik if he was home in the evening.

We ate at the big dining table in the room we jokingly called the best room, which was really only used on special occasions or when we had guests. An inherited crystal chandelier hung from the ceiling, casting sparkling rainbow-colored reflections around the room when the sun's rays caught it, but on this Saturday there was no sun. It was mild and overcast, but Mom had set the table beautifully, with lit yellow candles and napkins decorated with Easter chicks next to our plates.

I don't remember much about the meal, although I expect I thought the food was delicious. It was the same kind of perfectly ordinary celebratory food that was eaten at the same time in many Swedish homes: herring, meatballs, chipolatas, Jansson's temptation, hard-boiled eggs cut in half and topped with a blob of mayonnaise, a prawn and a sprig of dill. I liked everything except the herring, and probably had several helpings.

After lunch Erik and I each received an Easter egg, filled with small candies and a rolled-up hundred-kronor note. It was a surprisingly large sum of money, and I immediately started fantasizing about what I could spend it on. Then I fetched a pile of Donald Duck comic books and lay down on the living-room sofa. After a little while

Erik came in, grabbed one of the books, and settled down at the other end of the sofa. And so we lay there with our feet side by side, enjoying our candy. I liked those times when there was still a sense of balance and equality between us now and again, when he stopped trying to emphasize the age difference and lowered himself to my level. Like during the Christmas holiday when we did a jigsaw together, one with lots of pieces depicting the map of Sweden. And it was Erik who had taught me to use my new cassette player. One day when I was sitting drawing and listening to a tape, I suddenly felt terrified when I heard a whispering voice between two tracks. "Hanna... Hanna..." it said slowly and eerily, then Erik called out in his normal voice: "Happy name day, you old mudskipper!" That was what he used to call me when we were younger, and I thought the whole thing was so funny that I played it to my friends. I was so proud of having a big brother who not only remembered my name day but also came up with a surprise for me.

Easter felt kind of heavy, somehow; we were full of food and lacking energy. It was an early Easter, the end of March, but the whole of the spring so far had been unusually warm. It was damp and mild and breezy, and as we lay there reading, the room went dark, the sky was suddenly filled with thick gray clouds.

"I hope it isn't going to snow!" I heard Mom say. She was worried about the crocuses that were in flower all over the garden. She and Dad were still sitting at the dining table, chatting and tucking into the small cheeseboard that always appeared at special dinners. Neither Erik nor I were interested in cheese.

"This one's cool," Erik said, holding up the comic book. I knew exactly what he meant. It was a long adventure where Mickey Mouse and Goofy were in London, and the reader could decide how the story developed by choosing between two options, then turning to a particular page. "Is it new?"

"Kind of. It's not one of your old ones anyway."

"I know that."

He was going out with his friends later, and disappeared up to his room for a while before shouting "See you later!" from the hallway. When I'd finished my book I went upstairs and rewound the tape to find out what had happened on the chart. It turned out that Paula Abdul had hung on to the top spot, but a new track had come straight in at number two—"This week's shooting star!" as the jingle informed me. It was Madonna's "Like a Prayer."

I'd seen the video the week before and it had made a strong impression on me, even though I didn't really understand what it was about. However, it was incredibly dramatic, with a burning cross and a black saint, beautiful scenes from inside a church with atmospheric lighting and a huge choir. There was something dark and ceremonial about it that appealed to me. I thought it was on a completely different level from other music videos.

I turned the tape over and went back to the beginning of side A, which meant I didn't have to listen to Kaj

Kindvall babbling away. The first few tracks followed on straight after one another without a break, then I had decided that a brief silence between tracks might be good, like on a bought tape. However, when I pushed down the record button for a few seconds between recordings I didn't get the silence I was after, but a loud rushing sound that was most unpleasant.

I wondered if there was a proper way of recording music from the radio, what older and more experienced listeners did when they were taping the chart. I thought I would ask Erik when he got home.

I

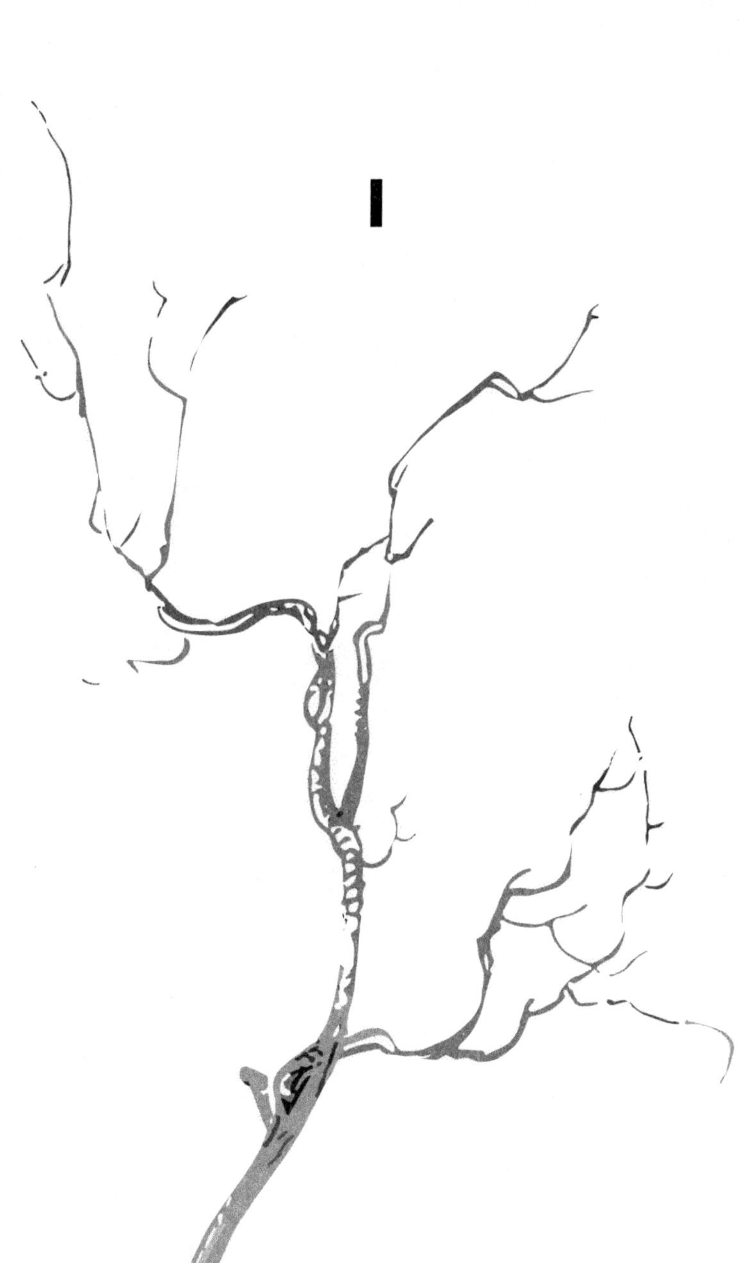

The forest went on forever, but there was a small part of it that was mine, and I knew it inside out. It reached from the residential area all the way up to the railway, where the tracks sliced deep into the landscape and divided it into "home" and "beyond."

The forest continued on the other side of the railway, beyond the high sandy banks covered in heather and fire-weed and wild strawberries, but I wasn't allowed to cross the tracks, and until Marcus moved over there I did as I was told. When my parents realized that the battle was lost, I was given clear instructions on how to look and listen at the crossing point. You could hear the approaching trains like a faint singing in the tracks long before they arrived. If the tracks were singing, you had to wait. If the tracks were singing, you could help yourself to the wild strawberries, which were bigger and more plentiful by the crossing than anywhere else.

Often when I was playing by myself in the forest I got the feeling that I wasn't actually alone at all. I couldn't put it into words back then, but it was a sense that something invisible was lingering among the trees, something that might suddenly appear, pick me out to reveal itself to. I got that feeling on those winter days when the snow was wet and the tree trunks were the deepest black, almost spongy, and if you scraped them you got damp, porous bark beneath your fingernails. Or when it began to freeze late in the afternoon, when the snow developed a crust, glowing orange in the setting sun and it was time to go home. Something within me wanted both to hurry home and to stay in the forest. Or on those hot summer days when the trolley by the railway crossing smelled of tar and warm wood, and I would seek out a patch of bracken where the soil was cool and moist and smelled like the root cellar. It was shady there even in the middle of the day, it was hard to see what might be hiding among the bracken's huge leaves.

I had to walk through the forest to meet up with Marcus.

Marcus and I got to know each other at the church's children's group when we were five years old. Even then there was a kind of mutual understanding between us, our personalities fit together seamlessly in a way that I immediately recognized as something special. Both of us had other friends, but I often felt ill at ease with the games the girls played. I didn't like the dolls' corner where they usually hung out, there was something cloying and unpleasant about all those frills and the pretend bottles and the plastic dolls with their creepy, staring eyes.

I knew that Marcus had the same intuitive distaste for the soft playroom that was the boys' territory—a room characterized by an explosive male violence that already existed within five-year-olds. On Thursday it was given over to the girls for a while, an early example of the struggle for equality, or maybe just a pragmatic child-minder's sense of justice, and I enjoyed being in there, jumping around on the thick, soft mattresses. The rest of the time I would never have ventured in there, the boys turned into a pack of wild animals, chasing one another, yelling, fighting with cushions, wrestling on the mattresses.

Marcus would sometimes spend time in the soft play-room while I sat in the communal area weaving brightly colored strips of plastic, but it always felt as if he went because of a perceived sense of obligation to the male gender. He actually preferred more sophisticated activities than jumping and shouting, and after a while he would come padding across the floor, pick up his loom, and join me. And so we would sit there in silence, totally at ease in each other's company.

Every day we all gathered together. We each fetched a green corduroy-covered cushion from a pile and sat down on the floor in a circle to listen to a story from the Bible. Then everyone was given a piece of paper illustrating the story of the day to stick into a yellow exercise book. The idea was that eventually the book would become a little Children's Bible.

Most of our group seemed to regard this session as an unwelcome interruption to their play, but Marcus and I enjoyed the stories. The burning bush had a great impact on both of us, and one day we talked about it as we stood side by side picking hips from a rosebush beside the sandbox.

"Burning bushes don't really exist," I said.

"If you believe in them, they exist," he said.

Even then I knew I wanted to have him around me for a long time.

At first Marcus lived with his mother in a terraced house in Krokek. Her name was Kristina but everyone called her Kicki. She was a hairdresser at a salon in the town center. She was a warm, pleasant person and it felt good to visit them. They had exotic things like cable TV and store-bought buns in the freezer, and a special banter that was fast and funny. No one ever mentioned Marcus's father, and it never felt as if there was a father missing in the house. Marcus and Kicki were their very own self-sufficient unit.

After a few years they moved to the other side of the railway. Kicki had met a guy, and they had a new house built, a big single-story place that was painted pale pink. They put up a cabin in the garden that was meant to be used for guests, but as time went by Marcus took it over. By that stage two little half-siblings had arrived and Kicki was still young—there might be more babies to come.

Marcus seemed to accept his new siblings with equanimity, but he was happiest when he was left in peace. There was a TV and a sofa bed in the cabin, intended for visiting relatives who rarely came, and a few years later the sofa bed was replaced by Marcus's own bed, along with a small desk and a chest of drawers where he kept his clothes. His stereo sat on top, and the walls were lined with shelves crammed with books. It was almost as if he'd left home.

I realized that he and his mom's new partner, Bengt, didn't get along particularly well, and I could understand why. Bengt was always jolly, waving his hands around when he talked, laughing loudly and often. He was nice, although there was a cheeriness about him that fit with Kicki's temperament, but not with Marcus's. Whenever we went into the main house to make a sandwich or get a drink Bengt was always pleasant to me, but there was something confrontational, almost aggressive about his positivity, and I often thought that if he lived with me, I too would have preferred to sleep in a cabin in the garden.

Bengt owned two burger restaurants, one in Norrköping and one in Linköping, and planned to expand. He would talk with enthusiasm and conviction about his desire to open a restaurant in every town in Sweden. Maybe it wasn't completely crazy, the one in Norrköping was very popular. The décor was 1950s-style and the staff wore turquoise uniforms with little hats and white aprons. There was a jukebox in one corner, and a striking neon sign flashing away outside with "The Burger King" written in ornate lettering. The food wasn't much better than McDonald's, and it was more expensive, but going to The Burger King was almost like going to a proper restaurant.

Bengt was something of a celebrity in both Krokek and Norrköping. According to the rumors, he came on to the waitresses, and whenever my parents mentioned him there was a certain skepticism in their tone, an attitude they adopted when talking about a certain type of person: those who talked too much, those who felt in some way superior. There was also something provocative about the pink house, a tasteless color everyone agreed, and an equally tasteless ready-built style of house. It had a huge bay window and two wings, the garden was flat with a perfect lawn that had arrived as great big rolls of turf, with a few spindly fruit trees that looked completely lost. At the front there was an extensive deck area with a white picket fence.

It was a strange location to build, up in the forest near the sand quarry. Someone like Bengt should have been living down in Sandviken with a sea view, and the fact that he rejected that possibility even though he should have been able to afford it was seen as further evidence of his general lack of taste and judgment.

Marcus was completely different from everything around him. He looked nothing like his mother, it was hard to believe they were even related. He once showed me a photograph of his father, a tall man with a serious expression and dark hair, and immediately Marcus seemed more firmly anchored in the world. His father lived in Malmö, and when we were older Marcus would go and visit him sometimes. He would come back with Danish candy, later with beer, and with a breath of the continent, a feeling that he was linked to the big wide world out there.

Sofia Samuelsson and I were sitting in her basement watching a video. We didn't have a video player at home, but Sofia's dad was interested in technology, and he was one of the first people I knew to get one. They had top-of-the-line speakers in the living room, and when her dad put on a record—often a dance band, sometimes Bruce Springsteen—the bass line pulsated gently through the entire house, like a heartbeat.

We were watching *Turner & Hooch*, a movie where Tom Hanks plays a cop who has a huge drooling dog, it was Sofia's mom who had rented it for the weekend, along with two other movies that we would probably end up watching too. I liked watching movies, it was a pleasantly undemanding pastime. We paid attention even to movies that didn't really interest us, because movies were a scarce commodity that shouldn't be wasted with idle chat. We could chat when the movie was over.

Sofia's mom had made us a big pan of popcorn and tipped it into a mixing bowl, sometimes our hands would touch in the bowl while our eyes were fixed on the screen. As usual when the movie ended I would say that I had to go home for dinner, and I would see a faint look of disappointment in Sofia's eyes and ignore it. I didn't want to go up to her room, because I knew what would happen: I would have to fend off all her questions by talking about something else, preferably identifying them before she was able to put them into words.

It was different with Marcus, his company was restful, almost passive, like when we used to sit side by side at the church children's group, undemanding in a way that hardly anything was undemanding, because even adults' supposedly undemanding care carried with it certain demands, or at least expectations.

Marcus and I didn't hang out much in school, even though we were still in the same classroom all day long. He spent recess with the boys and did whatever boys do when they are eleven, twelve, what was I doing, standing around talking about something meaningless, trying to avoid any questions about myself and about Erik, occasionally I would accept an invitation to someone's house, mainly because I couldn't keep coming up with excuses: if it wasn't Sofia Samuelsson it would be Sandra, who lived in the new development down by the stream in a light, airy apartment that smelled of cat litter, or Jenny, who lived in a terraced house near the school with a loom in the basement and earnest parents who belonged to the Pentecostal church. They all wanted me as their number one, a privilege I handled carelessly, because they always came second as far as I was concerned, second after Marcus. Maybe they saw me as I saw Marcus, unattainable in my lack of interest in fitting in, making myself dependent on others. They tempted me with candy and confidences, but with everyone except Marcus it always ended the same way, sooner or later: "Tell us about when Erik disappeared."

Erik had been determined to get confirmed long before it was time to do so. The fact that there would be lots of presents involved didn't seem to be his main motivation, as far as I could tell confirmation was really important to him, and even though I was a child back then, with only a vague idea of what the ritual meant, I thought I understood why. I enjoyed our end-of-semester celebrations in the church, the organ and the hymns, they were atmospheric and ceremonial in a way that hardly anything else was. When you were going to be confirmed you were invited to the priest's home, and I was curious about that too: the yellow rectory was impressive, almost like a small manor house, and I often wondered what it was like inside.

The night of Easter Saturday was special in the church, with midnight mass. Erik and four of his friends had decided to go, as one of their obligatory attendances before their confirmation. He had talked about it over breakfast that Saturday morning, spending time in the church in the middle of the night, with candles suddenly being lit and the organ playing. I imagined that something of the drama in Madonna's "Like a Prayer" would manifest itself in the church, with burning flames and a magnificent choir.

"Do you need a ride?" Dad asked.

"No, we're all going on our bikes," Erik replied.

They had gone to David's house and had a few drinks beforehand. Not enough to appear drunk when they showed up at the church, just a couple of beers. They all needed to rack up a certain number of attendances before their confirmation, and maybe it felt exciting and a little bit taboo to turn up slightly tipsy.

I thought they were probably overcome by the situation afterward. I pictured them standing on the path leading to the church, which was lit with flaming torches for the occasion, and deciding that the original plan—to go to David's father's garage, watch a movie, and maybe drink more beer—now seemed pretty banal as they had witnessed Christ's resurrection. And that one of them suddenly said: "Let's go to Mount Verity."

I was just a little girl when I first heard about Mount Verity, just like everyone else. The stories had been passed on from child to child for generations, spoken quietly when the adults weren't listening, even though the adults knew the stories too, and there wasn't actually anything that needed to be kept secret.

The mountain was past the zoo, next to the road leading to Kvarsebo. It was part of the long escarpment that formed the spine of Kolmården and gave the landscape its dramatic character—dark forest ending in steep gray cliffs, a wall of rock straight down to the waters of Bråviken.

Mount Verity was tall, with a flat top—a kind of plateau—that was perfect for picnics, the view was spectacular, but what really made the mountain special was the cave. There were plenty of caves in the area, even in elementary school we learned that Kolmården had been a hangout for robbers in the olden days, when the forests formed dangerous and barely passable barriers between different parts of the country, and anyone wishing to travel on the main route south from Stockholm was forced to go through Kolmården forest. The robbers stashed their booty in the caves, there were rumors of hidden gold that had been left behind in several of them, even though no one had ever found so much as a single coin.

The Mount Verity cave was different. It wasn't known as a robbers' hideout, but for having been used during the witch trials in Östergötland at the beginning of the seventeenth century. Just as in many places the authorities had determined whether a woman was a witch or not by throwing her into water, here they had used the cave. They lowered her down and asked if she had practiced witchcraft. If she answered yes, she was hauled up to face her punishment, and if she answered no she was left in the cave to try to get out on her own, which was impossible without assistance. If no one came to her rescue, she would eventually starve to death down there.

According to some stories, it was still possible to see scratch marks on the walls of the cave, left by women scrabbling to escape. However, others claimed these were not scratch marks at all, but natural variations in the rock, and no proof of the tales about the witches had ever been found, no remains, no traces. Then the interpretations of this version diverged: some said this meant that the cave had never been used as part of the witch trials. Another interpretation, the one preferred by children, was that nothing had been found because the women didn't die in the cave, but disappeared into the mountain, were swallowed up by it, leaving no trace behind.

"It's almost as if the mountain is alive," someone said.

Apparently you could hear women's voices echoing on Mount Verity in the evenings, muffled whispers from those who remained within the mountain and wanted company.

Over the years many had tried to find out exactly what went on in the cave: bold children, overconfident teenagers who wanted a bigger kick than a game of Truth or Dare. I would never have had the courage to get involved, but new stories emerged at regular intervals. Everyone had heard about the gang who had lowered someone into the cave, then those up at the top had shouted a question, and they all knew it was safest to answer truthfully, otherwise the person down below would suffer the same fate as the witches. If they lied, the mountain would take them.

I was generally a rational soul, but the stories about Mount Verity made me uneasy long before Erik disappeared.

And so they went off to Mount Verity on their bikes and mopeds, it would have taken maybe fifteen minutes in the darkness along Kvarsebovägen. In the summer the road was often congested, especially in the mornings when slow tourists towing camper trailers and heading for the zoo would be waiting to turn left into the huge parking lot. But on a night at the end of March, the road was deserted. No one saw the boys, no cars met the little caravan on its way to the mountain. Erik was cycling, he had his Crescent with its racing handlebars, pale blue with a metallic finish, it was a lovely color, almost the same shade as his eyes. He could ride fast with apparently very little effort, he would arrive with no sign of exertion apart from two bright red patches high on his cheeks.

They had parked their bikes and mopeds on the edge of the forest and set off among the trees. It was almost one thirty in the morning and they didn't have a flashlight, but the clouds had dispersed and the moon illuminated the route like a floodlight, leading them up to the mountain—it had been full just a few nights before.

From that point on, the stories about what happened varied. Three of the boys claimed that Erik had been with them so far, but Adam wasn't sure. They had scrambled up the mountain, sat down on the plateau, and drunk beer. It must have been beautiful, with the cold moonlight reflected in the dark waters of Bråviken—you could see for miles from up there, the whole of the flat Vikbolandet peninsula, to the east the silhouette of the nuclear power station at Marviken, to the west smoke rising from the chimneys at Bråviken paper mill, and beyond it the sky shimmering in the apricot-colored glow from the town.

They had continued drinking, but they all said afterward that it was strange they had gotten so drunk, because they hadn't consumed all that much beer. Were they actually drunk? Adam said he had felt kind of groggy, soft and woozy, while Jens described a feeling of intense anxiety, he had thought that the roots of the pine trees on the mountain were moving, trying to grab a hold of him and keep him there.

They all had difficulty remembering how long Erik had been with them, when he had left and how. David said he could barely recall riding home, he had woken in his bed on Easter Sunday morning with no memory of how he had gotten there, his head was pounding and he had only vague mental images of the previous night.

"There's something seriously weird about that place," he said.

The police searched the forest and dragged the waters. Bråviken is difficult because it is so deep on the northern side, where Kolmården ends with steep rock faces going straight down into the bay, it was easier with the lakes on the other side of the road. A helicopter circled over the forest, searching both for Erik and for anything out of the ordinary: a clue, a lead. Search parties were organized, people wearing high-vis jackets, their expressions grave as they made their way through the trees, police dogs were brought in and given one of Erik's T-shirts to sniff. The sound of the telephone sliced through the empty house, followed by quiet, serious conversations: they still hadn't found anything.

The interviews with Erik's friends were of no help at all. In their group of five I had always had the feeling that there was an internal hierarchy, that David and Daniel made the decisions, with a self-confident, kind of hard aura that made me stay out of their way. They were sports guys, used to choosing their team, used to being in charge. I thought Adam and Jens were nicer, their eyes were kinder. They would chat with me when they came to pick up Erik for some activity. Erik didn't seem to have a natural companion within the group, which sometimes made me feel sorry for him, but it didn't appear to bother him, at least not as far as I could tell. At the same time, I felt it was unsurprising that Erik was the one who had gone missing. That according to some grotesque logic he was the most superfluous, the one they could do without.

They all gave the same account of getting to the mountain, but after that they didn't know. In spite of this it was decided that there was no reason to suspect them;

once the forensic examination was completed, there was no evidence that a crime had been committed. No sign of a fight or any kind of conflict, nothing to suggest they might be hiding something. In addition they all seemed deeply affected by the gravity of the situation, aware that they had to tell the police everything they knew. But none of them had anything to add.

There was no snow that Easter, and no more throughout the spring. The crocuses in the garden were replaced by daffodils and narcissi. The weather was strange, mild and damp and windy, people talked about the weather while thinking of other things, the whole community held its breath and hoped that there would turn out to be a simple and understandable explanation. An accident, or an unhappy and confused fifteen-year-old who had taken his own life. Both would be a tragedy, of course, and that was exactly what people would say, "Such a tragedy," in serious voices, but at the same time they would be relieved, relieved that the tragedy hadn't affected them personally. A passing villain, which was one of the theories doing the rounds, would have been more alarming. A traveling kidnapper, murderer, pedophile, some sick lunatic who just happened to be passing that particular spot at that particular moment: that would involve a terrifying arbitrariness, that would mean it was sheer bad luck that Erik had disappeared rather than someone else. Worst of all would be a local perpetrator—one of them, someone they knew or at least knew of, or what if it were an unknown person who was still walking among them, a threat hovering over the forest and the houses and the water? The whole community was hoping that such a threat did not exist, that they could continue picking blueberries and organizing orienteering competitions and letting their children go out to play without needing to worry. The whole community hoped that whatever had happened to Erik couldn't possibly happen to them.

We ate quick-cook macaroni and ready-made meatballs, which was very unusual. Maybe I was the only one who actually ate, with a twelve-year-old's raging hunger that demanded food even in a crisis.

My maternal grandmother came to stay with us so that she could take care of me while Mom and Dad shuttled back and forth between our house and the police station. Her cooking was slow and old-fashioned, she made meatballs too. We would sit opposite each other at the kitchen table with the radio playing quietly, and when it was quarter to five and the news was about to start, she would switch it off.

I heard the crunch of car tires on the gravel drive when I had gone to bed, the serious voices in the hallway when Mom and Dad opened the door and Grandma came to meet them. The police still hadn't found anything.

When Mom and Dad came into my room to say goodnight, I pretended that I was already asleep.

And then I slept. Mom and Dad took sick leave from work, but it was considered best for me to go to school, best for my everyday life to continue as normal, even though nothing was normal and I didn't forget that for one second even if I was in a classroom. I used to go into the toilets, lock the door and look at myself in the mirror, meet my own erratic gaze and try to hold it. *Maybe I still have a brother, maybe I don't,* I thought, trying out the idea without it really finding a foothold as anything other than a quiet, nagging uncertainty.

Then I slept away the afternoons when school was over, which meant I couldn't sleep at night, on the weekends I slept until someone woke me and I felt as if I could have slept for several days if no one had woken me. Sleep was a wonderful state of freedom from the world, freedom from my thoughts. The very best time was that brief period between sleep and wakefulness in the mornings, when I was simultaneously aware and unaware. I was aware in the sense that I understood I had a body that was lying in a bed, but unaware because my brain had not yet updated itself with regard to reality, but existed in a kind of limbo where I could have been a small child, or it could have been a different season. Erik could still have been lying on the other side of the wall decorated with his music posters from *Okej* magazine, and the picture of a whale's majestic tail rising high above the surface of the ocean.

Then consciousness would catch up with me like a series of rapidly falling dominoes. Erik was gone, they still hadn't found anything, Erik might be dead, but as long as no one had found him he might still be alive, with every day that passed without anyone finding him the chances diminished, someone had to find him soon, because before long it would be impossible to keep on hoping and then we would have to start hoping that they would find him dead, because above all we wanted him found, we wanted this incomprehensible state of affairs to end. But for the time being it went on. And today it was still going on.

One afternoon on my way home from school I suddenly realized that I was standing outside my former childminder's house, on the paving at the bottom of the steps where I had stood so many times after school when I was younger. My brain had mixed up the schedule even though I was awake, followed a reflex from when I was in elementary school, and I was embarrassed and ran away, I felt stupid and caught out even though it was unlikely that anyone had seen me.

He could still be found alive. He could still be sitting on the porch one day when I got home from school, that was how I used to picture it. Like one time back in the fall when he'd forgotten his keys and was sitting waiting for me. Or he'd be sitting at the kitchen table when I got home, like he did on Thursdays when he finished earlier than me. Flicking through a magazine, drinking O'boy chocolate milk, and eating sandwiches.

Or the police would phone to say they'd found him. He'd broken his leg and couldn't make his way out of the forest. He'd managed to drink from a stream, but had eaten nothing but a few berries, so he was pale and skinny, gaunt. He would recover quickly, lying on the sofa with his leg in a cast, which I was allowed to draw on. My name in bubble writing, a palm tree, a heart.

"No hearts!" he would say, pretending to be annoyed, and we would both know that he wasn't really cross with me for drawing a heart.

Or he would call us himself. From a phone booth far away, on a crackly line from Stockholm, Gothenburg, Copenhagen. He had caught a train there all by himself. It wasn't like him at all, but it made more sense than the alternatives. It was something, at least.

Everything would soon be back to normal, I told myself, because that was what always happened. Life strived for normality, normality was that it was normal.

Or they would call and say they'd found him dead. That was the final possibility. He would have stopped being Erik and become a body in the forest, a body I wasn't allowed to see because it wasn't a pretty sight, that's what they said when they thought I wasn't listening, but Mom and Dad had to go and identify him, like on TV. He no longer existed, but there was a body to bury, there were rituals to be carried out, a pattern to follow, a time to stop waiting and start grieving. There was a normality in the incomprehensible, an incomprehensibility that was suddenly possible to share with others.

In the evenings I thought about what others were thinking. I imagined that all over Kolmården, and Norrköping and Östergötland, maybe all over Sweden, there were people who had heard about his disappearance on the radio, or read an item in the newspaper. The search for fifteen-year-old Erik from Kolmården is still ongoing. Erik is around five feet eight inches tall, with blue eyes and blond hair. At the time of his disappearance he was wearing a green jacket, a gray T-shirt, blue jeans and blue sneakers.

I thought there must be children lying in their beds at night, as I lay in mine, picturing his face, his family, his life. Imagining what could have happened to him and thinking the worst, then feeling a surge of deep gratitude that it wasn't their brother who had disappeared, that this had nothing to do with them, and I wished I was one of them.

I spent the evenings in my room, drawing. I began by tracing the girls in the *Starlet* magazines that I'd bought at the Salvation Army rummage sale, then I drew them freestyle so many times that they kind of became imprinted in me, as easy to get down on paper as writing my name. Then I started to construct my own girls, using elements from the ones in the magazines, and eventually they began to live their own lives. I made up stories about them, simple comic strips that were first about their fabulous hair and tiny waists, and second about their troubled love lives, something I didn't yet know much about, so I was able to get involved at a safe distance.

The psychologist I was sent to was very interested in my drawings. She was an expert on dealing with trauma in children, a pleasant woman with honey-blonde hair in a pageboy cut, and a large piece of bronze jewelry around her neck, I liked her jewelry very much.

"Drawing and painting can feel good when something difficult has happened," she said when I told her that I drew in the evenings. She assumed I was drawing something to do with Erik. Boys disappearing in forests and caves. Her disappointment was palpable when she saw what my drawings actually portrayed, that they were banal in every way, both in form and content, a million miles from the darkness you might expect from someone in my situation. My brother was missing and I was failing in my role as the traumatized sister.

Eventually the search was called off. There was probably nothing strange about that, after all they hadn't found anything even though they had gone through the forest over and over again, in wider and wider circles. But Mom couldn't accept that they had stopped searching. She and Dad still hadn't returned to work, and in the mornings she would drive up to Stavsjö or Ålberga or Fjällmossen or wherever she had decided they hadn't looked properly. She wandered around the forest all by herself, calling out Erik's name. Her voice grew hoarse, she came home in the evenings with her scruffy blue woolly hat covered in leaves and pine needles, she would tip the last few drops of cold coffee out of her Thermos and silently shake her head.

I didn't dare tell anyone but Marcus, because I was afraid it would sound as if she'd gone crazy. Maybe she had. Maybe all three of us had gone crazy, in different ways. Dad had never been particularly talkative or boisterous, but now he became even quieter, more introverted, sometimes almost closed off. He and Mom weren't in the habit of quarreling, I could only remember a few odd occasions during my childhood when they had snapped at each other, usually due to stress or tiredness or financial worries, maybe one had yelled because they thought the other wasn't doing enough around the house. But now they argued in a kind of contrary way, I heard Mom yell "Why don't you say something!" at Dad, but he didn't say anything, and the fact that she couldn't even fight with him made her even more angry. And of course she wasn't really angry, she was sad, or however you might define that feeling, just like Dad was, not just about Erik, but because they were walking beside each other, both equally paralyzed by grief, but incapable of coming together within their sorrow.

We were all alone, it was terrible to realize that that was how life worked. That anything could happen, and when it had happened it was impossible to predict the consequences, which was almost as horrible as what had happened.

I remember that spring as sticky and messy. People came and went in our house, pleasant, proper, always serious. I remember small details, fragments: the map of the Soviet Union in my geography book and the photograph of a great big harvesting machine driving across a huge cornfield. In the Soviet Union agriculture is often run collectively in so-called kolkhoz. "The Queen of the Night" by Haakon Pedersen had competed to be Sweden's entry for the Eurovision Song Contest, the lyrics were in *Starlet*: Sing to me, Bohème and Rigoletto / Sing to me, my life is your libretto. I liked the words even though I didn't know what they meant. At Marcus's house they had a whole box of Dumleklubbor chocolate-covered toffee lollipops in the pantry, because Bengt was able to buy candy at the wholesale price. Marcus would go down and fetch handfuls, and when I had eaten the lolly I would chew on the stick until the sodden wood splintered in my mouth.

Summer came and we went on the vacation that had been planned and booked before Erik disappeared, a long car journey to a cottage in Skåne where none of the three of us who remained knew what to do. One of the bedrooms was left empty because the cottage had been rented for four people, and immediately it was the same as at home: the empty room radiated an oppressive energy that weighed down the entire house.

We spent most of our time sitting outside, partly because the weather was glorious and partly because it felt easier to forget everything out there, the walls by the seating area were covered in honeysuckle and the garden had a sundial on a stone pillar that looked like a chimney, Dad showed me how to read it. We went to the beach in Falsterbo and it went on forever, it was the longest beach any of us had been on, and I thought that when Erik came back we must come again. That was when I still believed he would come back. I thought he would be surprised at how shallow the water was, we would wade out together and he would laugh in amazement, Dad would shout: "You'll soon be halfway to Denmark!"

But there were still only three of us, an awkward constellation that had never existed before. It must have reminded Mom and Dad of what it had been like before I was born, although now I was the only child, not Erik.

My brother was missing and I was the girl with the missing brother. From the perspective of a child I thought it was news that quickly grew old, but I soon realized that adults around me had a different view. A year and a half passed between Erik's disappearance and my transfer to high school, and to me that was an ocean of time, a period where the immediate shock and grief became normal and life went on, it was two summer vacations and an entire academic year and I thought that should have washed me out, wiped me clean in the eyes of others, made the anxious looks and tone of voice on the part of the adults superfluous.

But everyone would continue to think of me as Erik's sister for a long time yet. To the teachers at the high school Erik's disappearance was still a recent event. Several of my teachers had taught Erik a few years earlier, and they looked at me in a particular way, gravely and sympathetically. I was booked in with the school counselor without having asked to see her, I found myself sitting on a bobbly green chair in her little office and trying to convince her that I didn't need her help with anything, that I had stopped sleeping all day, I was coping fine with school and I had friends.

At first my story seemed to have raised my status with the other students, some of them came from the other two schools in Kolmården and had never met me before but still knew exactly what had happened. There was a mixture of curiosity and sensationalism in the corridors, which meant that for a brief period at the beginning of the semester I was welcomed in all camps. The social order had been shaken up by the allocation of students to new classes, and I could probably have sought out anybody, adopted the mindset of being popular and achieved it, but when it became clear that I had no desire to give them what they wanted, more and more of them withdrew, and I was soon back where I started: a few dutiful friends, but the only fixed point was still Marcus.

I knew there was speculation on the part of both children and adults. More than once someone asked me straight out what I thought had actually happened, I always answered evasively, said I didn't really have any idea.

But at night, before I went to sleep, my brain would start whirring, going over and over those parts of the course of events I was aware of, replaying the afternoon and early evening on that Easter Saturday when Erik called out "See you later!" and left the house for the very last time. I pictured him during midnight mass, cycling to the mountain, walking through the forest, the moonlight shimmering on the water from the top of Mount Verity.

What happens to a body in the forest? Someone finds it. It was hard to get lost in that part of the Kolmården forest, in order to do that Erik would have had to head north, cross Kvarsebovägen and continue up into the forest, toward the border with Södermanland, up to the marshy ground of Fjällmossen or inland, up toward Stavsjö. They had searched there, brought in dogs, without finding the slightest trace. It was considered unlikely that he would have set off on foot, they said, and if he had done so against all expectations there would have been signs, but there were none.

What happens to a body in the water? In Bråviken it would presumably drift straight across the bay to Vikbolandet, get caught among the reeds in Svensksundsviken and be found by some unfortunate angler. Or drift inland, past the expensive houses in Lindö and into the city. Or drift out to sea. To Gotland, to the Baltic. Dead bodies float, I knew that, but there is a limit to how far they float, and no one is going to find a body at the bottom of the sea.

What happens to a body in the mountain? To a person in the mountain? Had they searched the mountain thoroughly enough? I thought that was what everyone was wondering but didn't like to ask.

It should have remained spring 1989 until everything was back to normal, but 1990 came along and then 1991, and I became a teenager and the world around me changed. Suddenly there were Pringles and commercials on TV and telephones that looked like hamburgers, it was as if the world had become modern at the same time as I discovered my sexuality, which meant that for a long time I regarded that too as something modern, something I was lucky enough to experience because I happened to be alive in the era when it was invented.

I decided half-heartedly that I was in love, so that I would have confidences to exchange with my female friends. The object of my affection changed regularly, and some of them almost became real, I hardly knew whether I was actually in love or whether I had absorbed myself so completely into my role that it had become real. I didn't know if my friends' tales of love were real or not either, or if high school was simply a kind of mass psychosis–like training in heterosexual coupling up. Maybe that's how reality works: you think you're supposed to behave in a particular way, so you do just that without giving it much thought. So without giving it much thought I announced that I was in love with Jonas Hansson in 9D and my friends listened sympathetically to everything I had to say on the matter, just as I listened sympathetically to them, interpreting every signal the object of their desire might have given them: a glance in the dining hall, a glance in the corridor, the apparently remarkable fact that he had passed the common room when we had a free period, even though he had a lesson at the other end of the school at that time. It could mean only one thing: he was interested too, and the only way he could channel that interest was by staking out the common room.

We lay on someone's bed listening to "To Be With You" by Mr. Big, which we'd all bought as a single, the room smelled of White Musk from the Body Shop and there was a heavy, viscous intimacy about the whole thing that I thought with hindsight could have spilled over right there in someone's bedroom, been directed toward someone in the room, toward the person who shared your confidences and combed your hair instead of toward some guy in ninth grade who probably didn't even know we existed. A wandering, homeless desire just waiting for someone who was willing to accept it. The heavy intimacy was a bubble that burst when it was time to cycle home, when darkness had fallen and the streetlamps had come on, shining down on the schoolyard, if there was a soccer practice in progress, the bright white beam of the floodlights lit up the field. Then it grew darker as I cycled through the newly built area down by the stream, past the playground, up the hill toward the forest.

Marcus had overtaken me both physically and socially when we started high school. Those elements that had been latent within him when he was only five years old suddenly came to fruition, he shot up in height and was suddenly tall and broad-shouldered, with his dark hair in a spiky cut. He was popular in school, not by being a part of the popular clique but by being independent. Everything about him signaled an almost deliberate lack of interest in what anyone else was doing, and because people always want what they can't get, this made him appear irresistibly attractive. He passed through high school like a shadow, he never seemed to feel compelled to join in any particular activity or to align himself with any particular group, but he was always welcomed if he did choose to do so.

Sometimes he would hang out by the fast-food kiosk or the gas station where large numbers of teenagers would gather in the evenings. Those who had money would buy candy or soda, or cigarettes, and that was where everything happened, where you smoked and tasted beer for the first time, that was where you got together with someone else. I never went there. I thought the whole thing was unpleasant, a kind of brazen display of the very worst of being a teenager, the plotting, the drama, the need to fit in.

But because Marcus went there occasionally he had information on what was going on, whether Robert and Josefin had split up or were back together, the fact that David Lundin's parents were getting divorced, and

Sandra Ekman had hooked up with a guy in Åby who had a car. He would report back to me as we lay at opposite ends of his bed, but he always left himself out of the narrative, so it was from Sofia Samuelsson I heard that Marcus had been making out with Anna Strandberg behind the kiosk. I never asked him about such things, and I never told him about my half made-up love interests, our friendship was both honest and dishonest at the same time, dishonest in order to protect the honesty.

Personally I was nothing special in high school, neither pretty nor ugly, not the smartest in class but one of the smarter kids, at the lower end of the social ranking but not bullied or an outsider. I passed by unnoticed, which was exactly what I wanted. Even though Marcus and I were in different social circles, he never seemed to be ashamed of me or to have any problem letting people know that we spent time together. Sometimes after a dance down at the community center he would give me a ride home on the moped Bengt had bought him for his fifteenth birthday, he even did it when he had a girlfriend, from the spring semester of seventh grade he always had girlfriends. He didn't discuss them with me but I still knew about them, and presumably they knew about me too, but clearly didn't regard me as any kind of threat.

We always hung out in the cabin at his place. We would sit at opposite ends of his bed, flicking through magazines and listening to music, sometimes he would head indoors and come back with a bottle of cola and some cinnamon buns.

There was a gravity in everything he did, which I interpreted as a grown-up quality. He wasn't interested in sports, not because he was bad at them, he simply didn't care. Instead he was interested in music and reading, he usually played The Cure on his stereo, they were his favorite band, occasionally we would chat about a teacher, gossip about our classmates, he would talk about the future, say that he was going to get out of Kolmården as soon as he could, go to London or to his dad in Malmö. It sounded impressively determined, but it made me sad; I didn't want him to go. He said he would work in a bar, an expression that I knew came from his mom, who often told us that's what she'd done when she was younger. I always thought that would be before he had his breakthrough, in whatever way that might be, probably in a band with other young guys who also wore black and liked The Cure, or maybe as a writer. He read a lot and made vague attempts to get me to read something he enjoyed, at first it was *The Lord of the Rings*, then Stephen King, Hemingway, Camus's *The Stranger*, Klas Östergren, and I dutifully read some of them but I knew they weren't really my thing. Maybe I was still unusually childish, or maybe even then I knew I didn't need any more stories in my life.

Just before the summer break our entire year group went on a field trip in town to visit the rock carvings at Himmelstalund, followed by a guided tour of the art gallery. I didn't really enjoy outings, anything that diverged from the normal pattern of things stressed me out. I always felt as if absolutely anything could happen, that all the rules would no longer apply. Everyday life was better, with its predictability.

I had never been to the gallery before, and at first I was disappointed that it wasn't more attractive, just a box built of bricks, not the temple to art that I had wanted it to be. However, as soon as I got inside I realized it housed treasures I could never have imagined. Marcus and I were in the same group and walked side by side carrying our small folding stools, ignoring everyone else's chatter. The guide asked us to stop in front of a large painting, and everyone made an enormous noise with their stools as they sat down. The thick gold frame surrounded a picture of four figures against a dark background.

"David Klöcker Ehrenstrahl," the guide said. "That's the name of the artist who produced this painting in the seventeenth century. He was from Germany but worked in Sweden. He is usually known as 'the father of Swedish painting.'"

The murmuring at the back of the group suggested that some of my fellow students had already lost interest. The guide cleared her throat.

"This is an allegorical piece," she said. "Does anyone know what that means?"

I knew what it meant but had no desire to speak up. No one else volunteered an answer.

"It means that the figures in the painting are not real people, but symbols of something else." She pointed to each of the figures in turn. "Can anyone guess what they might symbolize?"

"Nakedness!" shouted Fredrik, who specialized in shouting things out.

"You're not too far away there," the guide replied.

She had dark hair and was young, maybe she was on a work placement from Linköping University. I saw Marcus glance at her and she glanced back. I was used to that kind of thing, everyone glanced at him, older girls did it all the time. He looked older than he was, as if he was already at college. I wasn't jealous, their glances meant nothing, they had no weight or significance. I looked at the painting instead. The guide pointed to the naked woman in the foreground, her blonde hair shining like a halo of light.

"She is naked for a reason. She represents *nuda veritas*, which is Latin for the naked truth. And what do you think the others might represent?"

"Time, maybe?" I said when I began to find the silence embarrassing.

The guide nodded encouragingly. "What makes you think that?"

"Because he has an hourglass on his head."

Someone sniggered, as if my comment might have been an attempt at a joke, but the guide looked enthusiastic.

"That's right. The hourglass measures time. Symbols like this have been used throughout the history of art to give paintings several layers of meaning. And who could this be?"

She pointed to a woman in a fluttering blue dress on the right.

Silence. Someone made a scraping noise with their stool.

"Justice," I said eventually, in a weary tone of voice.

"Exactly. And how do we know this?"

"Because she has a set of scales at her feet."

"Exactly!" The guide pointed to the scales. "In art justice is often symbolized by an old-fashioned set of scales like this, with two weighing pans. When they are evenly balanced, something is just. And who is the woman in the background?"

That was harder to work out, so I didn't say anything. Neither did anyone else.

"Wisdom," the guide explained. "She and time are lifting the cover from the truth together, can you see? And look at the motifs on the cover. It is full of snakes and other horrible things. You can almost think of this painting as a rebus, a picture puzzle. So what is the message?"

Once again, no one had anything to say. The guide looked at me.

"Well," I said. "I guess time and wisdom . . . are revealing the truth? Which leads to justice?"

She nodded. "Exactly. Fascinating, isn't it?"

"Can we go now?" Fredrik shouted out.

"Okay," the guide said with resignation in her voice. "You have fifteen minutes to wander around on your own and take a look at the collections."

Everyone except me was on their feet before she had finished the sentence. They folded their stools noisily and raced up the stairs. Soon there was only me left in the room in the basement of the gallery, somehow this was obvious from the atmosphere, the way the sounds from outside were muffled, the way that light was dim even though the walls were white. The windows were small, set high up just below the ceiling. I looked at the figures in the painting again. None of them were looking at me, they were all gazing down at the naked woman, she was looking up at an angle, with an expression of amazement, or anticipation. *Nuda veritas*. Out in the light at last.

Marcus was waiting for me in the foyer, where the teachers were trying to count us before we went back to the buses.

"Come with me, I want to try something," he said.

"Try what?"

"Just come with me."

He went over to Ulla Engström, our English teacher, who was standing just inside the main door with a list in her hand.

"Me and Hanna are staying in town," he said.

She looked at him in surprise.

"Staying? And how will you get home?"

"We'll catch a regular bus later."

It was clear that she didn't like it, but she couldn't be bothered to argue, so she simply said that the school's responsibility ended if we left the group, and that obviously we would have to pay our own bus fare home, and had we informed our parents? Marcus assured her that we had. He was a good liar, he always sounded so sure of himself.

I could feel the others watching us as we walked past the hired buses and across Kristinaplatsen, continuing beneath the lime trees on Södra promenaden. Their leaves were already large, and the whole town was turning green, there was lush, intrusive growth everywhere. It was a warm day and there was mist in the air, everything felt carefree, easy, I could smell exhaust fumes, freshly baked bread from a café, and everything seemed to combine into the essence of freedom, the city, possibilities.

Marcus wanted to go to Vaxkupan and look at records, so we strolled toward Nya torget, excited that his plan had worked. It was dark and cozy inside the store, with no other customers. Marcus began flicking through the new arrivals with a practiced hand. I felt a bit lost, I wandered over to pop and rock and started flicking too. I had just gotten through A and B when Marcus shoved an album in front of me.

"I'm going to buy this for you," he said.

The sleeve was ugly, in shades of brown, with two people kissing each other. It reminded me of a picture from the 1970s, and I thought everything reminiscent of the '70s was old-fashioned and horrible.

"Why?"

"Because I think you'd like it."

"There's no need."

"It's cool. I'm going to buy a few for myself as well."

I didn't understand how come he always seemed to have money, but maybe his dad sent him envelopes full of notes from his life in Malmö, to compensate for his absence. Or it might have been Bengt, who was perhaps also trying to compensate for something, for the fact that his presence in Marcus's life had made Marcus move out to the cabin. Or maybe it was both.

Marcus went back to the new arrivals section and picked out three albums, which he placed on the counter along with mine.

"I'll take these, please. Those three in one bag, this one in another."

He turned to me.

"Let's go get something to eat," he said.

It was still full daylight outside, so the neon sign above The Burger King wasn't as impressive as at night, and the place was barely half full. We sat in one of the booths, there were laminated menus in a holder on the table. Unlike other burger joints there was table service at The Burger King, which felt sophisticated. The jukebox was playing music at a low volume. Marcus handed me a menu.

"Choose whatever you like."

"Are you sure?"

"I'm not paying," he replied with a small smile.

When the waitress came over we each ordered an expensive selection: the burger of the season, which was large and included cheese, bacon, and some kind of special sauce, along with fries and two different dips.

We ate more or less in silence. Marcus picked up his yellow bag from Vaxkupan and started looking through the liner notes of one of his new records, so I did the same, trying not to leave greasy marks on the black-and-white photos of the members of Suede, all of whom wore serious expressions and were staring straight into the camera.

"You knew a lot of stuff back at the gallery," Marcus said suddenly.

I shrugged. "I've read quite a bit about art."

That was something of an exaggeration: I had read one book about art, an overview of the history of painting that I had taken out of the library several times, and I had spent more time looking at the pictures than reading, but I had done so thoroughly. I had acquired a certain amount of knowledge about the different epochs, what distinguished each one and the order in which they followed one another, and I had snapped up a number of words I liked. *Stilleben*—still life. Renaissance. Allegory.

"You never said," Marcus replied.

"It's not exactly something to show off about."

The waitress reappeared and Marcus ordered us both a milkshake for dessert.

"It's because we live in Krokek," he said when she'd gone. "Where nobody understands anything. It's different in Malmö. It's even a bit different here," he added with a sweeping gesture that encompassed Norrköping. "But it's better in Malmö. And Stockholm, of course. That's why I'm going to leave."

As usual I felt a stab of pain somewhere deep inside when he said that. I knew I couldn't protest, and I didn't want to be the person who did that, I didn't want to be the boring friend who wanted everything to stay exactly as it was even if that was how I felt, because anything else would mean that he would disappear. And above all I didn't want to be that person in front of him, because I knew he was attracted to the other kind, to those who encouraged adventure, who sought it out.

"I'm going to leave too," I said.

He nodded. "Of course you are."

That summer I often spent the evenings in my room, leafing through the book on the history of art and listening to the album Marcus had given me. The first time I played it I thought the music was weird, almost unpleasant. A metallic guitar, a discordant male voice, both somehow shining clean, yet there was something unique about the whole thing, something with the same color as the sleeve, like swimming beneath the surface of the brown water of a mountain lake with your eyes open, or like secretly doing something shameful.

Then I started to like it. It was dark and beautiful and horrible at the same time, it was different from anything else I had ever heard, and liking it seemed almost taboo. I thought it was a kind of music that only certain people would appreciate, and I really wanted to be one of them.

Summer twilight fell outside the window, but I hardly noticed. It was winter in Holland in 1565, people were skating on the frozen canals while three huntsmen returned from the forest with their dogs, the snow around them was heavy and damp, I had trudged through the same kind of snow a thousand times in the forest, on the way to and from Marcus's house, I had seen the same black tree trunks, the same black birds.

Mary was visited by an angel, his wings resembled a bird's, with feathers of deep red, pale green, creamy white, matte gold, the room they were in was bare, with a chalk-white vaulted ceiling and columns, it was beautiful, simple but perfect.

In Los Angeles someone had just jumped into a swimming pool and the water splashed up from the surface in white cascades. And yet it looked frozen, such a living moment motionless forever, there was something ominous about it in spite of the carefree milieu, the palm trees, the clear blue sky. You can't stay beneath the surface for too long. You have to come up soon. But no one came up.

August was the season of the yellow flowers. The sunflowers stood like gangly bodies with heavy heads along the fence at the back of the house, down by where we parked the car there was a profusion of tansy with its powerful scent, and goldenrod, a leftover from the time when our plot had been part of a farmyard, it was a long time ago, in the '60s. An eternity had passed since then, the farms had been replaced by residential areas, but the goldenrod had clung on through the decades, into the '90s.

The flowerbeds in town were resplendent with black-eyed-susans, deep yellow with a sooty black eye, still glowing as the darkness of an August night began to fall, the air was heavy with the sweet smell of freshly fried donuts. The carnival procession with its many visiting samba troupes had already made its way through the streets, danced along Drottninggatan among local residents in a variety of costumes, while a group of cheerful teenagers threw small packets of Stimorol chewing gum to the crowd. The packets lay around everywhere afterward, both empty and unopened, when I was younger Erik and I had gathered up as many as we could, more than a hundred altogether. Neither of us had needed to buy gum for months.

The following week we were due to go back to school, and there was a kind of restless energy among the crowds of people drifting around, an itchy feeling that this was our last chance, that whatever was going to happen during the summer had to happen tonight, because after tonight it would be too late. After the carnival procession had fallen silent, the heavy bass beat pumped out from Axel's Funfair, and from the beer tent, which was packed with those who were old enough.

We drank beer down by Strömmen instead, hidden behind the fishing club's lodge. Per's older brother had bought it on our behalf, and I thought it was revolting, so revolting that I could hardly get it down. The others laughed at me, they were more used to the taste. Then Per produced a half bottle of vodka too, and even though it was even more revolting, I took several big gulps. It seemed more rational, more efficient. Less torture for a greater reward.

I was drunk before the fireworks started. I had progressed rapidly from the initial pleasant wooziness in my head to something weightier, darker. The others were laughing and babbling away, I found it hard to keep up with their conversation, and I didn't really want to. It was suddenly difficult to sit upright, I lay down on the dry, prickly grass, turned my face up to the late summer sky. My body was so heavy. I would never be able to move it again, that was very clear. I would have to lie here forever, but that wasn't so bad, there were worse places. However, I should have settled down with my legs in a better spot, there was a stone under one thigh, but that was just the way it was and I couldn't do anything about it. The others' voices were distant now, as if I were underwater, they talked and talked and it seemed as if it went on for hours. I heard someone say my name, felt them tug at my foot for some strange reason, I couldn't be bothered to protest.

Then I saw Marcus's face above mine.

"Hanna!" he shouted.

I didn't know where he'd come from or why he was shouting. He hadn't been with us earlier in the evening, I didn't even know he was in town, but suddenly he was right here.

"Why are you yelling?" I said, but no words came out of my mouth. Were my lips even moving? I tried to touch them in order to check, but my arms were too heavy, I couldn't lift them.

"Hanna!" he shouted again, waving his hand in the air in front of my eyes, it was irritating, I blinked at him several times. At least I think I did.

"What's she been drinking?" he asked the others.

"Beer," I ventured, but I don't know if he heard me.

"Beer," Per said too, I couldn't see him but I heard him clear his throat.

"Just beer?" Marcus said.

"And this," Per replied, he must have shown Marcus the empty vodka bottle, he sounded embarrassed.

"Hanna?" Marcus said again.

His face was so close to mine. All at once the sky behind him exploded in a cascade of shimmering silver stars, slowly raining down in the darkness before disintegrating with a crackling sound. It was a perfect image. It was the most beautiful thing I had ever seen.

"Beautiful," I murmured, but no one could hear me above the noise of the fireworks. The sky sparkled—red and blue and green and gold.

"What? What did you say? How are you feeling?"

I couldn't answer, because a wave of nausea overwhelmed me with no warning. I rolled over onto my side and vomited violently into the flowerbed next to the lodge. Marcus gathered up my hair and held it behind my neck until I was done. By then the fireworks were over too, and there was a weird silence all around us.

"Sorry," I whispered.

I could smell gunpowder, it hung in the air like a light, unreal mist.

He gave me a little smile. "Just don't do it again," he said.

I couldn't stop thinking about him after that. The image was seared into my brain: his dark serious face so close to mine, lit from behind by a sky full of exploding stars.

It made me think of a picture of a saint, or a Renaissance portrait, like one of the paintings in the art history book: an image so self-evident that it seems as if it has always existed. As if it has lain dormant in some kind of collective subconscious until someone decided to paint it one day, and everyone who looks at it, throughout the ages, consciously or unconsciously, will think: "Oh yes, this picture." As if it had been missing from the world until then, and its arrival was a restitution that made the world whole.

In my fantasies I leaned forward and kissed him. I had thought of it before, many times over the years, but never as an actual possibility, never as something that could leave my brain and happen in reality. We had a different kind of relationship, a relationship by which I had set great store: I was nothing like those girlfriends who followed one another in quick succession, and he was nothing like my stupid imaginary crushes. I had been able to rest peacefully in the knowledge that what we had was something unusual, something worth taking care of.

But now it was no longer possible to rest. It was horrible to see him in school, surrounded by girls who presumably also lay in their beds at night thinking about kissing him, and maybe some of them actually got to do that, which was an even more unpleasant thought, bordering on unbearable. I stared at him in class, gazed at his perfect hairline above his black T-shirt, thought about touching his dark hair, pushing it back from his face, thought about him holding me, his arms around my waist, his hand finding its way beneath my top, my head buzzed and burned, I couldn't think, and yet I had no choice, and it made my whole body ache.

Dusk was falling earlier now and the forest surrounded the houses like a black silhouette that evening. When I set off along the track between the trees, and the streetlamps disappeared behind me, it took a little while for my eyes to adjust. Then I saw everything clearly. The ground was familiar, soft with pine needles, almost giving way beneath my feet, the roots of the pine trees polished by all the other feet that had passed over them through the years. The air smelled damp, from the moss, from the ferns, like an exhalation from nature. I saw the trunks, the track, the stars up above where there was a gap in the trees for the railway. I stopped at the crossing, there wasn't a sound. No trains approaching from either direction.

The gravel at the crossing made a particular crunching sound when I walked over it, muted and almost metallic at the same time, it was a sound I had always liked. It existed only here. It existed only when I was on my way to Marcus's house.

I hurried up the slope on the other side, the ground immediately became sandier, a premonition of the extensive sandy area beyond the trees, no more than a stone's throw away. We used to play there when we were little, me and Erik. Or was it me and Marcus? I remembered how difficult it was to scramble up the steep sides of the huge sandbanks, how your feet sank with every step, you had to move fast or you slid back down again, and it was hard, but the faster you were, the easier it was to get to the top. I remembered someone's hands pulling me up the last bit. Then we sat at the top, gazing out at the desertlike landscape spread before us. Fireweed in the sand, it was a pretty sight. Fuchsia pink and Naples yellow. Or ochre. I still had a great deal to learn about colors.

From some distance away I could see that the light was on in the cabin, and when I knocked on the door he opened it in seconds. He was wearing a T-shirt and his hair was a little tousled, he looked surprised, somehow defenseless. Faint music came from inside, and warm air drifted out into the chilly evening.

"Hi?" he said.

"Hi."

Maybe he somehow saw it in my eyes, because when I leaned forward and kissed him it was as if he had been expecting it, had known it was going to happen and simply wondered when. I had never kissed anyone before and yet I knew exactly what to do, it was fascinating, as if it was programed into my body, and once I had started I couldn't stop. A memory from when I was little suddenly flashed through my mind, when Erik and I were out one winter's evening and turned our faces up to the dark sky. It was snowing, and it was hard to distinguish the snowflakes from the stars, everything was shimmering before my eyes, the entire universe seemed to be tumbling down toward me. I had just learned certain basic facts: stars are suns in galaxies far away, it takes millions of years for the light to travel through space, some stars might already have gone out by the time their light reaches the earth. It felt like staring into eternity.

Erik and I were standing just outside our house, with the golden light from the hallway and the kitchen falling gently onto the blue snowdrifts, and I knew that Mom was making dinner in there while Dad watched the TV news headlines, and soon the annual Advent Calendar television show would begin. It was like standing at the intersection between two worlds, where one represented absolute security and the other was the very definition of the unknown, a perfect balance between the familiar and the dizzyingly unfamiliar.

Afterward Marcus walked me down to the railway crossing. Together we listened for singing in the rails, but there were rarely any trains at this late hour. Then I walked across the crunching stones, across the track, into the forest.

Often when I was walking home in the evenings it felt as if the pine trees gradually began to creep closer, the darkness seemed to expand and reach out for me, but tonight it was different. Tonight nature took me in her arms and held me, gently and tenderly, rocked me into a state of tranquility, as if I was at one with her and she was at one with me. We were both part of the same thing, my being flowed into nature and nature pulsated in my veins, it felt as if something had been completed.

From then on we often spent whole evenings in the cabin. Sometimes we began by drinking coffee, studying, chatting, sometimes that was all we did, like two well-brought-up children, on other occasions we suddenly found ourselves pulling off each other's clothes without really knowing how it had happened or who had taken the initiative. The windows steamed up, the air became stuffy and smelled of bodies.

He always looked me in the eye with a steady gaze, spoke in a calm, controlled voice for as long as he could, even when the passion took over. Everything we did seemed perfectly natural, like an extension of what had always existed between us, a grown-up continuation of something childish. Even when he held on to my wrists so tightly that I was left with bruises and had to keep my sleeves pulled down in order to hide them, it felt like nothing more than proof of our total intimacy.

The best part was that while it was going on, nothing else existed—including me. For a little while I could stop being me, stop thinking, stop feeling anything but what he was doing to me at that moment.

I used to think it would go on forever. That we would grow old—thirty, forty, fifty—and what we had would last, like a world of our own, a state that time could not touch. That was before I knew very much about time.

The day we finished ninth grade there was a party down at Kullaplan in the evening. The stream that flowed all the way through Krokek passed by there, lined by a row of weeping willows. It might have been the only place in Kolmården where they grew. I thought they looked magical, shimmering in shades of silver as if they had come straight out of a fairy tale.

Marcus was wearing a suit, and unlike most of the other boys he didn't look as if he was in fancy dress. He had brought a blanket, and we sat pressed close together, the June evening was chilly. When he asked if I was cold and I nodded, he took off his jacket and gave it to me, then put his arm around my shoulders and held me.

I hardly dared breathe for fear of destroying something. It felt like a movie. A public declaration that we belonged together. We drank white wine that Marcus had brought with him, in small plastic cups that he had probably stolen from the school restroom, and soon other members of our class came to join us, attracted by the wine and curious because we were suddenly letting everyone know that we were together. No one came straight out and asked a question, it was simply accepted as a new and self-evident fact, and I was immediately absorbed into an entirely new community of people who hardly even spoke to me in the corridors in school, but who were now more than happy to be in my company.

A few kids from another class were standing smoking a short distance away. Albin, whom I usually avoided, had made himself popular by being loud and obnoxious. He was Erik's friend David's younger brother, and had the same hard aura. He was surrounded by a group of girls who in spite of this—or maybe because of it—wanted to hang out with him. They were laughing raucously.

"Marcus!" Albin suddenly shouted. "So what's the Burger King doing tonight?"

His tone was sly, the others sniggered quietly and expectantly.

"Sorry?" Marcus was immediately on the defensive, as if he could sense where this was going.

"You do know what Bengt does in the evenings?" Albin took a step closer to us. "Well, everyone else knows. He fucks his waitresses while your mom sits at home. Is that what he's doing tonight?"

Marcus was on his feet in a second. Before anyone realized what was happening he punched Albin right on the nose. Albin staggered backward, taken by surprise both by the blow and its accuracy.

"What are you doing, you fucker!" he yelled. "I'm going to fucking report you!"

Blood was pouring from his nose, it was brighter than I thought it would be, an almost vivid shade of red, it looked unreal. Kajsa and Maria rushed over with a bundle of paper napkins to stem the flow.

"You have to pinch the bridge of your nose to stop it bleeding," I heard one of them say. Albin wasn't listening.

"You're fucking crazy, both of you!" He fixed his gaze on me. "Do you know why your brother disappeared? Because everyone else knows that too. Everyone knows he climbed down into the cave and lied when they asked if he was a fag."

Marcus immediately raised his fist again.

"Shut your mouth," he said quietly. "Shut your mouth unless you want me to beat you to a pulp."

It was a light early summer's evening, the sky slowly turned a darker shade of lavender. We knocked back the rest of the wine as we walked across Långa gärdet, where the cow parsley's flowers covered the ground like a gossamer veil, everything was so delicate, a slender new moon above the meadow, a slender new moon above Bråviken when we reached the former steamboat pier and sat down right at the end. Only then did we start talking properly.

"Is it true what he said about Erik?" I began. "I mean, is that what people say?"

"I have heard people say that. Not any of the boys who were there that evening, and I don't know if anyone actually believes it, but yes, some people say it anyway."

"You can't disappear into a mountain," I said. I'd told myself that hundreds of times, maybe thousands.

"I know Bengt screws around," Marcus said. "And I know that Mom knows, but she kind of goes along with it. Or pretends it's not happening. I presume she doesn't want to go back to the way things used to be. We never had any money, and of course she has Victor and Amanda now too."

"How did you learn to fight?"

He smiled. "I've been training. Bengt has a punchbag in the garage. Sometimes I pretend it's him I'm beating up."

"You can't disappear into a mountain, can you? Tell me you can't disappear into a mountain."

"You can't disappear into a mountain," he repeated obediently, but I didn't think he sounded entirely convinced.

There were so many questions, but no one to ask. Strangely enough the number of questions didn't diminish over time, they simply multiplied, and I realized that the older I got, the more there was to understand. I both did and didn't want answers to everything I was wondering about, the things I was afraid to think about, but maybe they could provide an explanation. Was there anything in what Albin had said? Had Erik's friends really been his friends, or was that internal hierarchy I had always sensed an indication of something more serious? A gang of boys who closed ranks against the one who was different in order to maintain the hierarchy, in order to avoid being tainted by the rumors about Erik, rumors that became the truth in school corridors and outside the gas station in the evenings.

And what if they weren't just rumors? What if there was a story behind them, an incident, maybe even a truth, one he couldn't share with his family, one he did everything he could to keep secret?

He never mentioned being in love, but what fifteen-year-old boy did back then? What fifteen-year-old boy would give his younger sister any clues at all about his emotional life?

How did he feel? Was he lonely? Was he depressed? Being bullied? Was there something he had wanted to share? Something he would have told me if we'd grown older together?

The questions just kept on multiplying.

Marcus turned eighteen on March 3, and the following day he took his driving test. One evening he turned up outside my house in his mom's gray Golf and sounded the horn until I went out and asked him what he was doing.

"I'm going to teach you to drive."

"I don't want to learn to drive."

"You should try everything at least once," he said.

"Is that your motto in life?"

"One of them."

I got into the passenger seat beside him, it felt unfamiliar, grown-up. Marcus looked pleased as we turned into Sjöviksvägen and drove past the Konsum and ICA grocery stores and the fast-food kiosk and the gas station where the high school students were hanging around with their bicycles and mopeds. It felt like half a lifetime ago since we were their age, even though it was only a couple of years. But now we were sitting here in a car.

The forest around us was dark as we drove along the road to the zoo. That was where everyone started learning to drive, in the parking lot. Several tall streetlamps cast their cold white light on the huge asphalt surface, which was deserted when we arrived. It was the middle of March, nature was still not showing much sign of the lush greenery to come, apart from a faint shimmer in the treetops, a sense that they were beginning to come alive.

The lesson went neither well nor badly for me. I managed to start the car after a number of attempts, then I drove slowly around a few concrete blocks.

"You need to try going a bit faster," Marcus insisted.

I already thought I was going pretty fast, but the speedometer was showing only ten miles per hour. I gently pushed down on the accelerator, thirteen miles per hour felt way too scary.

"How am I ever going to be able to drive at a proper speed? Like on a freeway? It's impossible."

"That feels completely different," he assured me. "You don't notice the speed in the same way, especially when everyone around you is driving fast too."

I did a few more circuits of the parking lot, it was pretty good fun, but at the same time it felt like a game, like driving a radio-controlled car in an amusement park.

"Next time we'll try a short run out on the road," Marcus said.

I shook my head, he smiled.

"You're not going to be one of those girls who never learns to drive. Move over."

We changed places, he drove out of the parking lot and turned right, onto a dirt track leading up to the forest.

"Aren't we going home?" I asked.

"I just want to show you something."

He pushed a disk into the CD player, it was slow, relaxing music with a heavy bass. He didn't listen exclusively to The Cure anymore, this was something I hadn't heard before but immediately liked, it was dark and soft at the same time. The trees were dense and black all around us, the car headlights illuminated the trunks of the pines as they swept by, a cathedral of gnarled columns.

You wouldn't want the car to break down here, I thought. *In the dark, in the forest. Or to run out of gas.* I glanced at the instrument panel and saw that the tank was three-quarters full, thank goodness. Nobody lived up here, and if anyone did, they wouldn't be the kind of person you would want to meet, some loner in a rundown old cottage, someone who was comfortable in the forest at night, who wasn't afraid of the dark.

The track climbed steeply, the gravel hitting the car's undercarriage with a metallic rattle. Eventually Marcus turned onto a narrower track, where we were met by a barrier with a whole collection of notices beside it. Protected area. No entry without permission. No photography or filming. Do not block the track.

"Where are we?" I asked.

"That's the TV mast," he said, pointing upward ahead of us. I looked up. It was dizzyingly high, the light at the top shone way up in the sky, high above the pines and firs. The Kolmården mast broadcast radio and TV to both Södermanland and Östergötland, I had seen it as a sort of gangly lighthouse throughout the whole of my life, far away on the horizon where forest and sky met, but I had never been close to it before.

Marcus opened his door and got out of the car.

"Come on."

"Where are you going?"

He leaned in and looked at me. "Closer."

I pointed to the signs. "It looks like they don't want us to do that."

"We can go a bit closer."

I undid my seatbelt, opened the door, and got out. Beyond the barrier, at the base of the mast, was a group of low buildings with gray metal roofs. It all looked kind of military.

Marcus had already ducked under the barrier and was marching on ahead, so I hurried after him. The exterior lights on the buildings lit up the ground as we got closer.

"There might be someone in there," I said.

"At ten o'clock at night? Do you think they have a mast keeper? Like a lighthouse keeper?"

Suddenly there was a loud noise farther away in the forest. We both jumped. A rapid banging, which stopped equally suddenly.

"What was that?"

"The wind," Marcus said.

"That's what people always say when they don't know what it is."

"It's usually the wind."

"I don't think it was the wind."

He smiled at me. "So what do you think it was?"

"I don't know."

He came and stood behind me, slipped his hands beneath my jacket and my top and placed them on my stomach. I gave a start, they were cold, I was surprised, it was a long time since we had done anything like that.

It was verging on unpleasant, but he kept his hands there until I had gotten used to it, and they were a little warmer.

"Is it horrible?" he said with his mouth right next to my ear.

I didn't know whether he meant the noise in the forest or the place or his cold hands, but it didn't matter, the answer was the same.

"A bit," I said.

He slowly slid his hands upward, they found their way under my bra and cupped my breasts.

"How about now?"

"A bit," I said again.

Marcus moved one hand back down, unbuttoned my jeans and slipped his hand inside. I was breathing heavily, so was he.

"How about now?"

"A bit," I said for the third time.

"But you like it when it's horrible, don't you?"

"Yes," I mumbled.

"Good," he said.

II

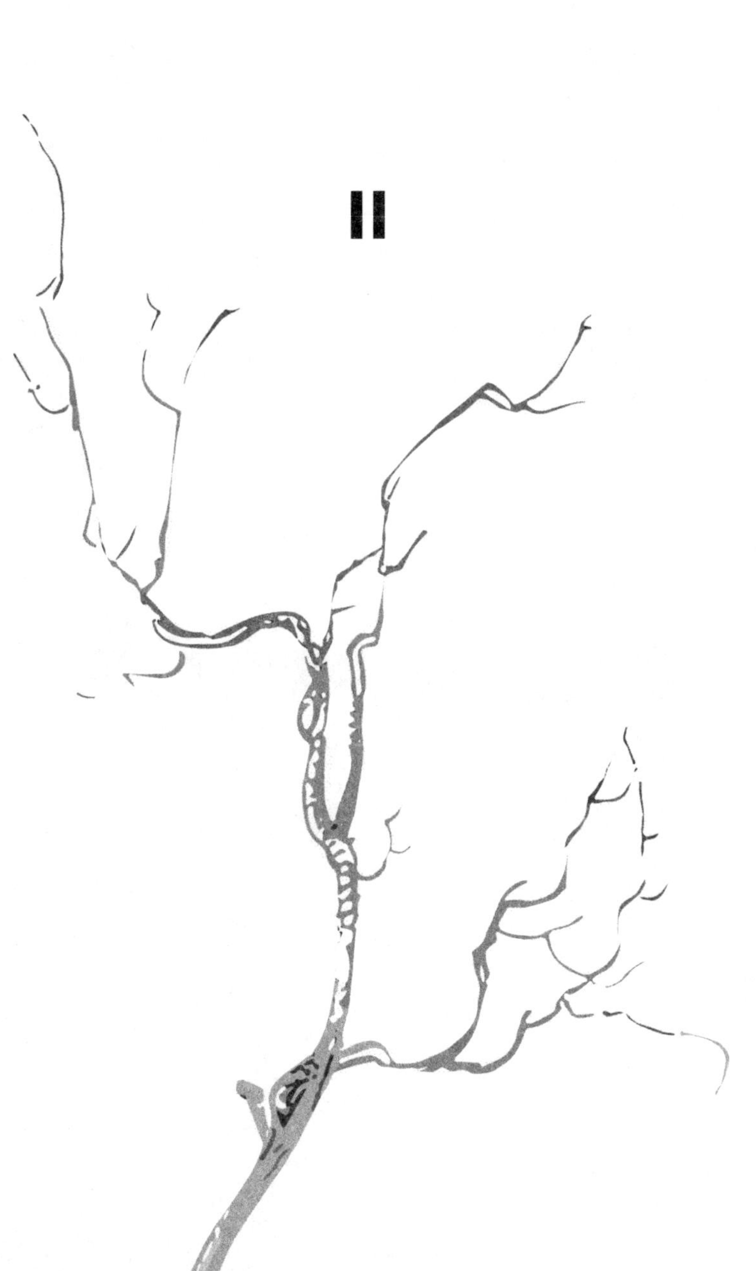

The sound in the large room was subdued, kind of muffled. There was a worn gray wall-to-wall carpet, and the ceiling was covered with spongy polystyrene tiles, tiles that absorbed the hundreds of telephone conversations that took place every evening between people who would much rather be doing something else.

I logged on to the computer. The system was old, the text large and pixelated, and the graphics were simple and clumsy, only two colors. I put on my headset, adjusted the microphone and clicked on the first call. It rang out for quite some time before anyone answered.

"Sundström," said a female voice.

"Hi," I said. "My name is Hanna and I'm calling from VQS, Vision Quest and Survey in Gothenburg. I was hoping to speak to Yvonne Sundström."

"That's me," she said in the slightly wary tone almost everyone adopted when I had introduced myself.

"Great! We're currently conducting an investigation into consumer habits, and you have been chosen at random to take part. So I was wondering if you have a few minutes to answer some questions?"

A few minutes was a deliberately vague statement, it rarely took less than fifteen minutes, sometimes twenty or more.

"Is it about how I vote?" she asked.

"No, we're looking into consumer habits and product knowledge. It's mainly concerned with groceries and household products."

"Do I get paid?"

"Unfortunately there is no payment for this particular investigation, but your answers are important for the statistical analysis."

This was a cunning formulation, designed to evoke a sense of obligation and responsibility, and I was slightly ashamed every time I had to come out with it. She sighed with an air of resignation. The power of the telephone was remarkable—older people seemed to feel that they had to answer and then cooperate when someone called them. Presumably things would soon change, when the sought-after consumers came from a younger generation with a more careless attitude toward the telephone.

"Well, I was just about to make a start on dinner, but . . . okay."

"Perfect. First question: How often do you eat jelly?"

She was silent for a moment, confused perhaps by the contrast between my formal introduction and the banality of the question.

"How often do I eat jelly?" she said suspiciously.

"That's right."

"Do you mean ordinary jelly? Like . . . strawberry jelly and . . . lingonberry jelly, that kind of thing?"

"Yes, ordinary jelly."

She laughed. "I guess . . . a few times a week."

"Would you say once or twice a week, three to five times a week, or more than five times a week?"

Another silence.

"Well, I mostly have it with my porridge, so that's maybe three times a week. So I'll go for three to five times a week."

"Excellent. So my next question: How often do you buy jelly?"

"I sometimes make it myself, but maybe that doesn't count?"

"This particular question is about jelly you buy from a store. But I bet your own jelly is delicious!" I added.

She laughed again. "Let's see . . . I'd say I buy jelly a few times a year."

"Would you say once or twice a year, three to five times a year, or more than five times a year?"

"I guess that would be three to five times as well. The children eat quite a bit."

"I understand. Now, what brands of jelly are you familiar with?"

She sighed. "Let me think . . . Bob, I guess."

I selected Bob from the options on my screen.

"Can you think of any other brands?"

"Er . . . Önos, maybe?"

"Önos, good. Any more?"

"Felix?" she said hesitantly. "Or is that mainly peas and that kind of thing?"

"I'll add it to the list. Any more?"

Silence. "Coop, I suppose, if they have their own brand? I'm not sure. And ICA too." She suddenly sounded enthusiastic. "And maybe Willy's? And Hemköp?"

"Perfect. Can you think of any more?"

She fell silent again. She really was taking this seriously.

"No, that's it I think."

"Excellent. Can you tell me what brands of jelly you've bought in the last fourteen days?"

"I haven't bought any jelly lately." She sounded a little defensive now. "We've just been eating the lingonberry jelly we've already got."

"No problem, I'll make a note of that." The fact that she hadn't bought any jelly meant that I didn't need to ask her what brand she had bought, which would speed things up a little. "Next question: what brands of jelly have you seen advertised during the last fourteen days?"

"Advertised . . . Do you mean like leaflets through the door?"

"We're thinking of all kinds of advertising. For example, leaflets through the door, ads in newspapers and magazines, on public transport, at the cinema, on TV or the radio."

She laughed. "I don't think I've ever heard jelly advertised on the radio!"

"No, maybe jelly doesn't come up too much on the radio," I said in a friendly tone of voice. "But how about the other types of advertising I mentioned?"

This time the silence went on for quite a while.

"I think I might have seen something on TV."

"Do you remember what brand it was?"

"These are difficult questions."

"There's no hurry."

"Can you help me out with some brands?"

Her desire to get it right was touching.

"I'm afraid I'm not allowed to do that. This investigation is concerned with what you have seen and what you remember."

She sighed. This was going to take some time.

"Think about the brands you mentioned just now," I prompted her. This was actually off-script, but I wanted to move on. "Have you maybe seen an advertisement for one of those?"

"I might have seen Bob advertised," she said eventually. "On TV4."

"Fantastic."

Neither of us said anything while I filled in her responses, then clicked through to the next segment.

"Is that it?" she said optimistically.

"Not quite. The next question is about ready-made and frozen pizza. How often do you eat ready-made or frozen pizza?"

It started raining as I headed toward Korsvägen. According to the display the number five was due in seven minutes, so I went into the newsagent's and flicked through a few magazines to pass the time. When the tram came rattling along, the rear section was full of young guys in expensive clothes on their way from Örgryte into the city as usual.

I usually tried to avoid walking to the tram stop with anyone from work, I hurried away quickly after the last call of the evening. Sometimes I failed, but if it was someone who talked so much that I didn't really need to contribute, it wasn't too taxing: Samir, who usually babbled about some new sci-fi movie, or Tilde, who would tell me all about the party she'd been to over the weekend and the party she was going to next weekend. It was more difficult if I ended up with someone who wasn't as chatty as them, because a conversation that demanded input from me was almost painful. After five hours on the phone my brain was anesthetized. Sometimes I thought it might have been different if the surveys I was conducting were about politics or social issues, if they were genuine opinion polls where people gave genuine, well-thought-out answers. At the same time, it was quite appealing to do something that didn't require me to think at all, to sit there almost like a robot typing in witless answers to equally witless questions. Sometimes I really got into it, regarded it as a challenge to lead the interviewees through the conversations, tease out the next product name, make them feel important. Maybe I ought to work in a similar field, I thought occasionally, but for real: become some kind of counselor, listening patiently to people struggling with their bad relationships, nodding and making appropriate comments, giving simple advice that was seen as meaningful, because people who ask for advice on that kind of thing are ready to believe that any opinion on their situation could carry a truth within it.

Vision Quest and Survey was a company where you worked until you found something better, or something you would rather do. Most employees were students just like me, sitting there for several evenings a week to supplement their student loan. Some were middle-aged or older, I felt sorry for them because the reasons why they were there were never positive. Some had lost a better job because of downsizing or disagreements, and hadn't yet managed to find anything else. One had suffered burnout and was easing himself back into work. One man who must have been in his fifties had worked there for many years, and still believed he would soon get his breakthrough as a composer. Most of this older group worked days, the shifts were longer and presumably quieter, because fewer people would answer the phone. My nightmare was that I would end up like them, that I would be sitting in the same staff kitchen in ten years, waiting for the career as an artist that had never taken off, working long shifts to pay for a studio that led precisely nowhere, but I couldn't let it go because that would mean the final failure. As long as I had my studio, there was still some hope of success.

The calls were generated at random by the computer, and every time I hoped that a man in Stockholm wouldn't answer. Men in Stockholm were just the worst—always stressed, often condescending. “Don’t you have anything better to do?” was a frequent question, and it always got to me. *Of course I have,* I would think, and then: *Do I really?* And I would get angry, because it felt as if they had won. I pictured their lives as a distant and exotic image of success, a fantastic career and beautifully ironed shirts, a suntan that lasted well into the fall, a big house and a wife and children, maybe a mistress, an impressive golf handicap, overseas vacations, and a rich social life with others who shared the same status in society. And then someone calls from Vision Quest and Survey in Gothenburg, making demands on their time to ask questions about their cell-phone contract, what a joke. “Fifteen minutes?” they would sometimes yell after they’d asked how long it was going to take, and of course I was lying anyway, because if they answered in a particular way there would be more questions, questions that would require them to fetch a pen and paper and write down support words and rate their phone operator. I always hoped they would say no to the survey, because if they said yes I would hear their frustration increasing after only a few minutes. Sometimes we had only gotten halfway through after the promised fifteen minutes and it was already seven thirty, they were having a barbecue, they were going out, they had to put the kids to bed. I would miss out a question or fill in the wrong answer to avoid the need for a follow-up question, always aware that a supervisor could be listening in to our conversation, I might be called in and told in a stern voice that I was endangering the statistics, and that if this happened again I might lose my job.

I was invited to a party at Tilde's on Saturday. I rarely went out with my coworkers on the weekend, the parties my fellow students organized were always more fun, but she had made it seem as if it were important to her that I went. Her apartment was on a street off Linnégatan, which made no sense at all to me. How could she live there, when she was studying and had a badly paid part-time job, just like me? Then I realized there were parents who could help out financially, that the hundreds of thousands of kronor that made no sense to me obviously didn't come from her job as a market researcher.

Tilde was studying Education and was going to be a teacher, which sounded stable and well-considered. I found it slightly embarrassing to say that I was doing an art foundation course, it sounded more like a hobby than something you could actually live on. Maybe I should stop thinking that was a possibility, and become a teacher too, an art teacher, it might even be enjoyable. Encouraging a particularly gifted pupil to pursue art, making a difference to another person's life.

Tilde provided box wine, Franz Ferdinand was playing in the living room, some people were already planning to go on to Pustervik later. Samir was talking to a girl I didn't recognize, maybe one of Tilde's fellow students, they were standing close together, closer and closer as the evening progressed.

I sometimes wondered when love would come to me. As if love were a resource that was shared out through the providence of someone else. Like the tax declaration form from the IRS or a summons to the dentist: if it didn't show up there must have been a hitch at a higher level where these things were dealt with.

I thought that was how it seemed to work, people around me got together in an almost mechanical way that maybe didn't always have much to do with love, it was more a sense of responsibility or duty, a need to fulfill the task of being part of a nice couple who enjoy long, lazy breakfasts on the weekends, go for a walk in the botanical gardens, measure a wall in order to put up a shelf they've driven to IKEA to buy. There was something irritatingly fabulous about this togetherness, and I often wondered to what extent those involved really wanted to be there. They didn't seem excessively happy, but they weren't unhappy either, they accepted their relationship with stoical equanimity: This is what you do, this is how you create a grown-up life. After spending several years doing everything to break away from exactly that kind of life, represented by their parents, they suddenly performed a U-turn and accepted that they ought to become exactly like them, accepting their money for the deposit on a place to live, buying their IKEA shelf, having cozy dinners at home instead of going out partying, maybe getting a dog, eventually upgrading to a child.

Personally I halfheartedly went back to someone's apartment from time to time, without imagining that it would generate anything other than a brief closeness, or lead to anything else. What did I want from life? It stressed me out that I didn't actually know.

I often dreamed of Erik at night. Sometimes we were children again, lengthy dreams with no clear action or content, when the endless summers of our childhood played out in my mind like idyllic postcards from the past: Erik and I trying to paddle a canoe, Erik and I picking wild strawberries in the cow pasture at Grandpa's summer cottage, our hearts in our mouths, Erik and I fighting for space on a Lilo in a forest pool, the warm, amber-colored water all around us, gray mountains and tall, straight pine trees lined up against the backdrop of a completely cloudless sky.

Sometimes the dreams were different. In one I was in the forest, on the track leading up to the railway, when a deer suddenly appeared in front of me. It looked straight at me, and I got the feeling that the deer was in fact Erik, that he had come back, in the form of a deer for some reason, but that didn't matter, the important thing was that he had come back.

"Don't go," I said, but when I cautiously took a step closer I trod on a twig that snapped. The deer stiffened for a second, then turned like lightning and fled through the forest.

In another dream I was at Mount Verity searching for him, and as I stood in the cave I saw an opening in one corner, with light pouring from it. *How strange that no one has seen this opening before,* I thought and stepped inside. I found myself in an enormous hall, like in a fairy-tale palace: columns and crystal chandeliers, gold and jewels, everything sparkled and shone. Erik was sitting at a table. He was wearing brightly colored clothes, he was older, and his hair had grown into a golden pageboy, the same style he had had when he was little. He looked like a handsome prince in a painting by John Bauer.

"Have you been here all the time?" I asked him.

He nodded.

"Won't you come home with me?" I said.

"I have to stay down here," he replied.

I always woke up with a strange feeling in my body, simultaneously sad and comforted, everything felt kind of woozy, like a slight hangover, and I would try to cure it in the same way: a long shower, coffee, a walk. But however far I walked I couldn't forget that I was the one who had been allowed to live, that I was walking around, I was alive, while Erik was still missing. *I ought to be more grateful,* I thought, *I ought to take better care of my life,* but how do you do that? I felt as if I had been tasked with living in a certain way so that justice would be done, so that this would somehow compensate for the fact that

Erik never got to grow up. It was a debilitating thought. Nothing I could do would ever compensate for that.

I ate at work on the evenings when I was there. I had a thirty-minute break, I would heat up a frozen ready meal in the windowless staff kitchen, where lamps hung from the low ceiling and spread their artificial light on the plants that just about survived in there, like we all did. I ate Findus cheese schnitzel with béarnaise sauce and fried potatoes, or rissoles with potato croquettes, herb butter, and cherry tomatoes. Both dishes were salty and greasy, with a few obligatory green beans. I often thought that I ought to make myself a packed dinner to bring in, I ought to start eating better, but it never happened. I also hated the idea of my coworkers taking an interest in what I had, with curious looks and comments. That's the way they behaved with one another, especially the slightly older colleagues who clearly cooked delicious and nutritious dinners and brought in the leftovers. It felt personal, private: as long as I ate ready meals, I wasn't responsible for what was in them.

If I was going straight home from my art class I often bought something tasty for dinner, usually from the Chinese restaurant on the way. It was like a throwback to Sweden as it used to be, with old men drinking beer and reading the evening papers in a big restaurant where I had never seen more than a handful of customers. A neglected aquarium stood in one corner, while a TV mounted on the wall was showing the day's lottery draw.

The man at the till recognized me and was always pleasant. I usually ordered chicken with cashew nuts, or occasionally a chicken dish flavored with ginger, maybe beef in a dark soy sauce with onions or bamboo shoots, it was perfectly ordinary food, delicious in a perfectly ordinary way that I liked. The portions were generous, there was always enough for at least two meals, so even though I was buying takeout pretty often, it wasn't really expensive.

I would sit at a table and leaf through *Expressen* while I waited, glancing at one or two album reviews. Then I would collect my bag containing the warm plastic boxes and cut across the square to my apartment. Winter was almost over and you could sense spring in the twilight now, it was cold outside, there were still gritty patches of ice on the ground, but the thin strip of light that clung to the horizon lingered for a little bit longer each day.

Home was a sublet in one of the big blocks on Wieselgrensplatsen. It was close to the tram stop and several large grocery stores, sometimes there was a florist's stall in the square selling cheap, lovely plants, I filled both the apartment and the glassed-in balcony with them because it wasn't particularly cozy, it was an impersonal mixture of IKEA and old stuff that seemed to have finished up there by chance, nothing really went together. And yet I was happy there, the location suited me very well: the big building on the modest square that had a small-town feel, it managed to be magnificent and unassuming at the same time, carefully and benevolently designed in the finest tradition of the Swedish welfare state.

Otherwise I wasn't too fond of Gothenburg, I thought it was oddly planned, a collection of different parts of the city randomly thrown together, a kind of limbo where you waited for life to begin for real, hopefully somewhere that wasn't Gothenburg. In fact the entire city was like an enlarged version of my workplace: a temporary stop on the way to something else. It didn't feel as if anything was really real in Gothenburg, I always thought: it's cool that you have a morning paper, but it isn't a real morning paper. Cool that you have art schools, but they're not real art schools. Cool that you have a city, but it's not a real city.

Hisingen was also a weird place, the suburbs were sort of eating their way into the city center but were hindered by a bridge that could actually be opened; if they wanted to they could stop us from getting into the city, raise the drawbridge and shut us out. Hisingen was city yet not city, it was intersections and suburbs and large grocery stores, a place to catch a bus that would take you even farther away, McDonald's at Backaplan shopping center that was a fragment of the real world, between old men boozing and parking lots and superstores.

My hallway was small and dark, I picked up the mail: mostly advertising leaflets, a bill, and then a window envelope that looked both formal and fun at the same time. The edges were decorated with a border of balloons.

"Where does the time go? It's crazy, right?" it said in a cheery typeface on the piece of paper inside. "It's ten years since you left high school, and to celebrate Reunions R Us are inviting you and everyone else who graduated from your school in 1994 to a party. A party that will go on all night long! With music from back in the day, of course—will you have the nerve to ask the person you had a crush on to join you in a slow dance this time?"

I didn't want my food to go cold, so I tipped one portion onto a plate and sat down at the table with the invitation in front of me. The party was to be held in the school dining hall, a simple three-course menu would be served, drinks at cost price, please inform the organizers of any food intolerances or allergies.

I was no longer in touch with anyone from Kolmården, not even Marcus. After graduating he had moved to Lund and I had come to Gothenburg, and we had stopped communicating. I googled him occasionally, he had already achieved a doctorate in theology. There was a small picture of him next to the presentation of his research on the university's home page, and he looked just the same, but older, more serious. He had written essays and articles with titles such as "Imagining the apocalypse—revealing the revelations of Nordic folk tales," and "Does God live in the forest? Animalistic features in 20th-century Swedish literature." It all looked very highbrow, it made me feel inferior to him in a way that I found frustrating.

Throughout high school I had thought that I would make something special of my life. It had annoyed me that many of my classmates had such a casual attitude, bordering on indifference, to the future at the age of fifteen. Didn't they have any dreams? My grades were good, I was going to study, move far away, maybe overseas. I would live in a place where no one knew who I was, where my life was not tainted by my past.

I often thought of the evening when Marcus and I were at The Burger King on Drottninggatan, when it felt as though we had sealed an unspoken pact. "I'm going to leave too," I had said, it was as if it became possible when I spoke those words. "Of course you are," he'd said, and we both did it, we left Kolmården, but for what purpose? Those who stayed probably had better lives than me, who couldn't get into a proper art school and spent the evenings asking people what brands of jelly they were familiar with. Not exactly something to boast about at a school reunion. I could imagine the surprise on their faces, the way they had to bite their tongues to stop themselves from saying what they were thinking: that they had expected me to be doing something considerably more impressive by this stage.

I had started running in the evenings, and as the spring progressed, I ran more and more. Every evening when I wasn't working, because there was nothing I liked more than spring evenings, and at the same time nothing I liked less. I ran to be absorbed by the atmosphere, the shimmering magic of the blue hour along the quaysides of Eriksberg, then through the residential areas where everything was bursting into life, a suburbia with rhubarb leaves like ears directed at space, perhaps the rustle of a hedgehog moving through last year's brown leaves, it was like running straight back to my childhood.

Running was a solitary pastime, anonymous in a way that appealed to me. It was one of the few situations where I felt as if I were no one. No one took any notice of a runner who was out when everyone else was out running too, and even though the quaysides and the shopping mall parking lots were busy in the evenings, I could run there without anyone paying attention to me, a body among other bodies, without a specific errand, with no goal other than to keep moving. I particularly liked mild, misty evenings, it was as if I became one with them, dissolved and became part of them, I turned up the volume in my earbuds and increased my speed, felt my heart pounding, felt the blood pumping through my veins, felt that I was alive.

At the same time it was those spring evenings I was trying to run away from, because they were revolting, the misleading hope of the lighter evening, the false promise that everything would return. Sometimes the memory of Erik seemed so distant that I began to doubt whether it had really happened. Whether I had actually had a brother. Maybe it was just something I had dreamed, an intense dream full of details, but a dream nevertheless. I had absorbed the memory, just as a mussel places layer after layer of mother-of-pearl over a grain of sand, I had buried it inside me, turned it into a hard, shimmering sorrow deep, deep inside. It was like an echo from eternity, a myth from ancient times, a whisper from space: Once upon a time I was a part of something else, something bigger. Once upon a time I was whole. Once upon a time I had a brother.

You could register on the Reunions R Us website to accept or decline the invitation, and once you had created an account you could log in and see who else had said yes. I found it ironic that they were using the most common mechanism in high school—peer pressure—to evoke the feeling that you didn't want to miss this party.

But it worked. I registered, still with the intention of saying no, I logged in and clicked around the site, which was way too aspirational for its purpose: a simple chat where you could talk to your former classmates, the opportunity to upload photographs from back in the day.

I wanted to see the list of those attending, and as I glanced through it I felt every bit as uncomfortable as I had expected, this was something old and grubby, something I had left behind and had no desire to return to. The same names that had surrounded me since elementary school, the same little world, the immediate feeling that absolutely nothing had changed.

And then I saw Marcus's name. That was what I had been looking for, of course, even though I hadn't expected to find it because he was the last person I could imagine showing up at a reunion. *Then again, maybe not,* I thought when it had sunk in. Everyone liked him, although no one had been really close to him. Our high school class didn't represent anything difficult to him, he would come along as a successful, maybe the most successful person in our year.

The whole thing stressed me out, put me in a bad mood. I quickly pulled on my running gear and set off, ran as fast as I could, through residential areas that looked exactly like everything I was trying to run away from. I found an extra burst of speed, but it didn't help.

There was an opportunity to see Marcus again. I could actually just send him an email, his address was on the university's home page. I could write that I'd seen he was going to the reunion, that I didn't want to go but it would be good to meet up again in a different context, maybe one day he would have a reason to be in Gothenburg, there were lots of conferences for academics, surely at some point someone in Gothenburg would want to hear him talking about his research?

However, I didn't want to seem too pushy. If he'd wanted to see me he could have gotten in touch, but I hadn't heard a word from him for years. Why did I want to see someone who didn't want to see me? To write to him and ask for an audience—that was demeaning. I had no desire to give him the upper hand.

But the thought that he was going to the party and I wouldn't be there was unbearable. I could picture him sitting there talking to all those other girls who had been in love with him ten years ago, they might even mention me, someone would ask "How's Hanna these days? Are the two of you still together?" and he would answer no, no, I haven't heard from her for a long time.

I turned up the volume in my earbuds, ran even faster.

Mom and Dad were sitting outside drinking coffee when I arrived. I went in and fetched myself a cup, they were still the same cups as when I was little, gray-beige Arabia porcelain in a heavy, clumsy '70s design. They ought to buy some new cups, nobody used this kind of thing any longer, except maybe in their summer cottage, or if they were really really old people. Mom and Dad weren't that old, they had another ten years or so to work, but something had happened to them after Erik disappeared, something had happened to the entire house. You could hear the loud ticking of the kitchen clock, you could hear it even if you went into the living room, because everywhere was so silent. Was it different before? Was the house lively and cheerful? Were they?

Nowadays Dad would answer with a resigned "It is what it is" if anyone asked how he was, a comfortable way of avoiding putting his feelings into words while conveying that he was carrying something dark, something broken, and it was as if those simple words together with the ticking of the kitchen clock draped a sticky, passively sorrowful veil over the entire house.

Could you hear the clock before Erik disappeared? I had no memory of the sound from when I was little, not until the evening when Grandma made meatballs for me while Mom and Dad were out searching for Erik. That was when the house fell silent. Time stopped and simultaneously became more tangible. Now there was food in the refrigerator that was well out of date, the last time I was home I'd found a jar of pickled beetroot that was covered in mold, the colors were vivid and looked artificial even though they were anything but: nature was taking its course. Rose madder and emerald green, like rotting jewels.

Mom and Dad seemed pleased to see me, although we quickly ran out of conversation. There wasn't much to say about my job, or art school. I still hadn't heard anything from the art colleges, I hadn't done anything special. The party was due to begin at six, I didn't need a ride, I would enjoy the walk. No, I hadn't heard anything from Marcus.

The dining hall was decorated with balloons, and was full of people talking and laughing loudly to make themselves heard above the music, it was Ace of Base just like at every high school dance. I quickly realized that those who were there from my class were mainly those who still lived in Kolmården, of course they were, why hadn't that occurred to me when I read the names on the list? There was Anna who worked at the ICA store and had children who were already in school, Robert who worked for a plumber in Kolmården, Sanna who worked at the day-care center and also had children, although they were younger than Anna's. They showed pictures of their kids, they talked about their houses: Anna's place had suffered damage from damp in the cellar during the spring, they'd had to dig up the yard to lay a damp course all around the foundations. Robert had been to Crete over Easter, he had a fantastic tan, his hair was almost as white-blond as when we were in high school. They obviously got together from time to time, if it wasn't planned they would bump into one another in a store in the town center, or at the pizzeria, or maybe at a parent-teacher conference, sharing updates on what had happened since their last encounter, agreeing to go to the reunion.

There was no sign of Marcus, and apart from Emma I seemed to be the only one from our class who lived anywhere other than Kolmården or Norrköping and had traveled here especially for the party. Emma told me she was studying civil engineering at the university of Örebro with industrial economy as her main focus, and there wasn't a single word in that sentence that interested me, but I did my best to make conversation with her, because somehow it felt as if I ought to do that, because those of us who had tried to make something of our lives should stick together, although when I told her what I did it was clear she thought I had more in common with the rest of our class.

I had quickly knocked back the glass of Cava that was served on arrival and I was desperate for another, but no one seemed to be offering refills, I wondered if I ought to make my excuses and leave before things got any worse. A moment later I saw Marcus over by the door. It really was Marcus, a little older, a little heavier, wearing a dark suit and a shirt and tie. I pushed through the mingling crowd and tapped him on the shoulder.

He seemed pleased to see me.

"Hanna—fantastic, how are you?"

He gave me a hug that was brief, almost fleeting, but it was enough to remind me of exactly how it felt to hug him, I remembered it with my whole body. He even smelled exactly the way he used to.

"Fine, how about you?"

He nodded and was about to speak when the music stopped and someone tapped on a glass with a spoon. Andrea from 9A, who was apparently acting as some kind of hostess, shouted "Hello hello!" Marcus rolled his eyes at me, the conversation around us died away. Andrea had clambered up onto a chair and was standing there clutching the glass.

"Okay!" she said loudly in her strong Östergötland accent. "For those of you who don't recognize me, my name is Andrea Johansson and I was in 9A, along with those crazy girls"—she pointed to a group over by the window, one of them waved to her—"and just like the rest of you, we don't look a day older!"

There was a smattering of laughter.

"It's great to see you here," she went on. "And I hope you'll have a fantastic evening. The food will be served shortly, so when I've finished speaking I suggest you go and find your seats. As you know there will be three courses, and after the meal we will clear away the tables together to give us a really big dance floor!"

Someone at the back of the room cheered, a few people clapped.

"The bar is over there," Andrea added, pointing to some tables covered in paper cloths, "and now I'd like to propose a toast."

She raised her glass, as did everyone else. Including me, even though my glass was empty.

"Here's to old friends! *Skål*!"

"*Skål*!" everyone responded.

Marcus gave me a slightly pained smile, I smiled back. The hum of conversation around us quickly picked up, someone put the music on again.

"I suppose we'd better find our seats," he said.

"I guess so."

I wanted to say something amusing but I couldn't think of anything, the tension was too great. How do you talk to someone you haven't seen for such a long time, someone you desperately want to talk to? It was as if every topic of conversation that came into my mind seemed too trivial, so we made our way over to the long tables in an awkward silence, and when we got there it turned out that he was sitting at one end beside Emma, who was training to be a civil engineer, and he immediately started chatting with her. From my place at the other end of the table I could see them laughing. Next to me, Robert and Jens were discussing the pool Jens was planning to install in his garden. I was already bored before the main course was served, which made me angry with myself, the problem lay with me, not them, why had I come to an event where the whole point was to be cheerful and have fun if I didn't want to do that? I was constantly on my guard in case someone asked a question about something I didn't want to discuss, which was virtually everything: What did I do, where did I live, was I with anyone, did I have children? In the worst-case scenario they would ask about Erik, and just knowing that I was in a situation where everyone knew what had happened to him made me feel stressed and defensive, and I had difficulty following the conversations around the table, I went to the bar several times in the hope that the wine would help me relax, but it didn't seem to make any difference at all.

Andreas Palmkvist, who was sitting opposite me, made an effort to converse politely about Gothenburg, which was sweet of him, he told me his sister had lived there for several years, so he had been there quite often, we both felt it was a city we didn't like even though it had similarities with Norrköping with its history of the working class and its trams, but we both thought Norrköping was better, we nodded in agreement, I glanced at Marcus hoping he had noticed, but he appeared to be deep in conversation with Emma.

It wasn't until after dessert, when most people were a little drunk and the atmosphere was more relaxed, that Marcus met my eyes when I looked in his direction. He held my gaze, took a packet of cigarettes out of his pocket and nodded toward the exit, I nodded back. And so we walked down the stairs and along the corridors together, past the lockers that had been orange ten years ago but were now pale gray and already covered in graffiti. We went past the common room, no longer quite so scruffy but equally depressing with its uncomfortable seats and terrible fluorescent lighting, out beneath the overhanging roof, which was surrounded by shadowy beds still sparsely populated with rhododendrons, and sat down on a bench.

Marcus gave me a cigarette and lit it for me. His hands looked exactly like they used to.

"So," I said. "What are you doing these days?"

"Why do you never get in touch?" he said.

We smiled.

"You could get in touch with me," I said, my tone a little sharper than I had intended. I was experiencing a strange mixture of emotions, jealousy, disappointment, yet I wanted nothing more than for him to touch me. I glanced at his free hand, thought he should put his arm around me, pull me close, make me forget everything the way he used to, make me forget myself.

He nodded.

"Absolutely. I'll check my schedule. I'm working on a doctorate in theology at the moment. In Lund."

I adopted a surprised expression, although I already knew that.

"Wow, cool! Congratulations, I don't suppose it's easy to get a research post?"

He shrugged. "So how about you? How did it go with your art?"

I couldn't believe I hadn't prepared an answer to that question—it was all I thought about.

"It's . . . To be honest, I don't really know. I'm doing an art foundation course in Gothenburg, but I'm hoping to get into a decent art school in the fall. I should hear soon."

I omitted to mention that this was the third time I had applied. I cleared my throat. "And I do a bit of part-time work, interviewing people over the phone."

"Like opinion polls?"

"No, it's mostly to do with consumer habits."

"Market research? About food, that kind of thing?"

I was embarrassed at how banal it sounded, especially compared with what he was doing. I felt like a child next to him. I might as well have stayed put in Kolmården, had an ordinary day job, maybe at the ICA grocery store like Anna, done a little drawing in the evenings, kept it as a hobby instead of having some stupid idea of making it my career. No doubt Anna had a good life, secure and well-ordered, she might not earn much money, but it would be cheap to live here, plus she had a husband who was some kind of tradesman, all the men around here seemed to be some kind of tradesman.

"What brands of soda and other alcohol-free carbonated drinks, so we don't mean beer, are you familiar with?" I said in my warmest telephone voice.

Marcus laughed. "Not beer?" He pulled a sad face. "How about cider?"

"Cider is fine, as long as it's alcohol-free."

"In that case I'll say Kopparberg and . . . Pripps, maybe?"

"Can you think of any other brand?"

"I don't really know much about cider."

"And if you think about soda?"

"Which soda brands do I know?"

"Yes."

"I mean, there are dozens of them . . . Are the people you call supposed to list every brand of soda they can think of?"

I nodded. "And then I ask them which brands they've drunk and which ones they've bought and which they've seen advertised. And we haven't even started on mineral water."

He smiled, shook his head.

"Shit, Hanna, I hope your art is fantastic."

His tone was jocular, but it didn't feel like a joke. I felt the prick of tears in my eyes, I blinked them away, I didn't want to appear oversensitive, but he noticed and his expression softened.

"Are you okay?" he asked.

I nodded, sniffed. "So how are your mom and Bengt?"

"Good. Bengt sold the restaurant a few years ago, and now he's bought a store supplying home electronics and computers instead, on Hospitalsgatan. He says he's going to open a chain of them. He and Mom still live in the same house. And how about you—did you . . . learn to drive?"

"Not exactly."

"I guess you don't have anyone to practice with."

"You're right—I haven't."

"They drive like idiots in Gothenburg."

He smiled. Was he with someone? Did he have a nice girlfriend who was also studying for her doctorate in Lund, maybe they lived together, put up shelves together on the weekends, maybe he was teaching her to drive. In a few years they would have children, move into a house. How come he had everything worked out and I didn't? It used to be the other way around. The whole thing felt like a betrayal, the fact that he had moved on, created a proper grown-up life. It was an entirely unreasonable reaction on my part, I realized that, why should he ask me for permission? We weren't even in touch. Soon he would finish his thesis and get a job at the university, just like his father. I had googled him too before the reunion, he was a professor in the history of ideas. It was strange that I couldn't remember Marcus ever saying what his father did, and strange that I had never asked. I had been satisfied with the knowledge that he lived in Malmö and looked a lot like Marcus, but older, I had assumed that he had an ordinary job, maybe he was a tradesman too, since he'd had a child with a hairdresser. But he was an academic, and Marcus was no longer the guy with a faded The Cure T-shirt, the guy in the vulgar pink house full of screaming step-siblings and a pretend-dad who was the Burger King—Marcus was an academic too, organized and well-dressed and grown up.

A group of people emerged from the school building for a smoke. Lovisa, who had been in our class, came to join us.

"I dreamed you two were together," was the first thing she said. She was talking loudly and slurring her words slightly.

"Did you?" Marcus said.

"Are you?"

He shook his head.

"We haven't seen each other for several years," I said.

"She never contacts me," Marcus said.

"He's too busy with his thesis," I countered.

Lovisa sat down on the bench and made a big performance out of lighting her cigarette.

"You two are the kind of people who everybody knows will stay together for the rest of your lives," she informed us. "We all thought so when we were in school. Hanna, you used to be so good at drawing, are you still doing it?"

"I am, actually. I'm at art school now."

She nodded. "I'm sure you're going to be a famous artist. Then I'll be able to say 'I used to know her! She was in my class at high school! And she was already brilliant at drawing back then!'" She laughed to herself, as if the idea had really perked her up. "Did you know I was with Danne for a while? Danne who was there when your brother disappeared. He often used to talk about it, he still felt bad about it. I'm sure he still does."

I didn't know what to say, but it didn't matter—she wasn't waiting for a response.

"I mean, he hardly remembered anything from that night, but he was absolutely certain he'd heard voices. Or whispering. He was sure there was something in the cave, or in the mountain."

"Yes, that's what the boys said. When they were interviewed," I said tersely.

"Do you believe them?"

"I don't know what I believe or think. I don't think anything. How about you?"

I heard the sharpness in my tone. I realized I was drunk too, it was as if all the wine suddenly hit me and my head felt as if it was burning, Lovisa's demanding expression was just the same as it had always been. That was how everyone used to look at me here, they all wanted something from me: an explanation, a theory, a reaction, anything to satisfy their hunger for something that was horrible but risk-free, the same urge that was satisfied by ghost stories and the most gruesome tabloid headlines, I was their fiction, an exclusive firsthand source for a tragedy that could safely be observed from a distance.

"I do think there's something there," Lovisa said. "You know, some kind of... I don't know, presence? And that's why they never found him."

"Lucky it wasn't Danne who disappeared," I said.

"It sounds kind of sick, but yes, of course I thought that at the time," she replied. "But then he had nothing to lie about."

She stared at me as if I ought to understand what she was hinting at, and of course I did, but I wanted to hear her say it.

"What do you mean?"

She shrugged, dropped her cigarette on the ground, and squashed it with her shoe.

"Well, if they were down in the cave... it's stupid to lie. When you know what can happen."

She got up to leave, I stood up too.

"So you're saying it was Erik's fault? That he disappeared? He had only himself to blame?"

Marcus had positioned himself beside me. "Let's go, Hanna."

"But the dancing hasn't started yet!" Lovisa protested. She seemed to have already forgotten what we were talking about. "Marcus, we were going to have a dance! You can't go yet."

I shook my head. "I don't want to dance," I mumbled as I turned away and set off across the schoolyard. It was still dusk, the sky was lavender-colored and the lamps outside the sports hall glowed orange, it was all so familiar, the yellow brick, the torn basketball hoops, the untidy shrubbery behind the cycle rack. I could hear Marcus's footsteps behind me.

"Hanna, wait." He placed a hand on my shoulder. "Are you okay?"

I shook my head. "How could I possibly think I could come back here? And that it would simply work? As if everything were normal."

"Everything is normal, isn't it?"

"Everything is absolutely not normal!" I said, I was almost yelling. "Don't you get it, I'm a complete failure! I'll never get into a decent art school, I was an idiot to believe I ever would, I might as well have stayed here, but that wouldn't have worked either, you can see that, because here I'm a fucking freak who had a fucking freak for a brother. But everything's worked out for you, so that's great. It's great that you're doing your doctorate, how wonderful."

"Are you angry with me, Hanna?"

I really was angry with him, because he was still making his way effortlessly through life, doing exactly what he wanted yet succeeding at everything. I succeeded at nothing, the fact that I'd thought I would was just embarrassing. The idea that I could become an artist, for God's sake, it's like a joke, who did I think I was? What a curse it was to think you were something. Why didn't I do something ordinary with my life, study industrial economics or whatever the fuck it was called at the university of Örebro, something useful like what Marcus's girlfriend was no doubt doing, his nice girlfriend, in his stupid, splendid little life in Lund, the whole thing was disgusting, it was disgusting that his hands touched her when they should have been touching me, I suddenly realized that the only thing I wanted, the only thing I cared about, was for him to touch me.

"Could you just . . ." I began.

"What?"

My whole body was itching, my brain was itching, it was like some kind of allergic reaction. The wine couldn't fix it, I knew I needed something else.

"Could you just take away my thoughts," I said quietly. "Like you used to. Could you just make me forget myself."

I recognized something in his eyes when I said that.

"Is that what you want?" he said.

I nodded.

"Then you need to ask nicely."

"Please," I said.

I was woken by the sound of the telephone ringing. When Erik disappeared, Mom bought a phone with big buttons and an extra loud signal, meant for old people or those with a hearing impairment. She wanted to be sure she never missed a call, and she hadn't lowered the volume since those days. The ringing sliced through the entire house. As no one else answered, I got out of bed and ran downstairs.

"Hi, it's Hanna."

I was hung over, the hallway was swaying as if I were on board a ship, my head was pounding.

"I'm calling from the police," said a male voice. "I'd like to speak to either Eva or Sören Hallman."

That couldn't be right. I had to say "Sorry?," but the voice simply repeated what it had said, briefly and firmly. It really was the police.

"I'll go and get them," I said quietly.

They were both outside. Mom had made the kitchen garden much bigger over the past few years, and she took good care of it, she was always out there weeding and thinning out and watering and pruning. It was a pretty garden, at the moment all the plants were small and spindly, but in summer there would be vegetables, herbs, berries, and lots of flowers providing generous bunches for the dining table well into the fall. She spent several hours a day working her magic.

"Telephone!" I shouted from the porch, but neither of them reacted. I slipped on my shoes and ran over to them. The sun hurt my eyes, it was way too bright.

"Telephone," I said again. "It's the police."

Mom got up slowly behind the bucket of weeds, turned around. For once she looked at me as if I had said something important. Then she quickly pulled off her gloves and dropped them in the bucket, hurried along the path and into the house, with Dad following silently.

I stayed in the garden, eagerly breathing in the fresh air, it cleared my head a little. It wasn't a remarkable garden, but I had always liked it. The vegetable patch, a few fruit trees, a toolshed, and a seating area at the back. Another seating area at the front, more fruit trees. Lilac bushes. There used to be a swing in the apple tree at the front when I was little, it was a large, old tree and I loved to sit on the swing watching what was happening in the street. Neighbors coming and going, a cat, the mail van. A small world.

In my head all the old scenarios played again, I knew them by heart at this stage. Erik was alive. It was incredible, but they had heard via Interpol that a man who might be him had been seen in Barcelona. Maybe he'd had a minor stroke, lost his memory, something that made him confused and disoriented, but he was alive.

Or he was dead. A group of walkers along the Sörmlandsleden trail had contacted the police after discovering what they thought were human bones when they left the trail and went into the forest. He was dead, he was a skeleton now, a grotesque clichéd image of death, like a symbol in a medieval painting, it was both incomprehensible and something concrete. We would be able to organize a funeral. It would be like in the movies, friends and neighbors coming by to pass on their condolences, bringing homemade casseroles and freshly baked bread, offering hugs and sympathy and well-meaning words, because when he disappeared, no one came. There had been no obvious time to come by, nothing to mark the point where anxious waiting gave way to grief, there was no reason to express condolences, so no one came.

I started to shiver, the air was chilly and I wasn't wearing a jacket, so I went indoors. Mom and Dad were sitting at the kitchen table.

"They've found a shoe," was the first thing Mom said.

"A shoe?"

"They think it might be Erik's."

Her expression was weary.

"Where did they find it?"

"In the cave."

"What?"

She nodded. "It was a family, they were having a day out over the weekend and they'd lowered themselves into the cave on a rope. They were playing some kind of game, hunting for treasure, but all they found was a shoe. Then the dad remembered reading about Erik's disappearance, so he called the police."

"But..." I began. "How can it have been in the cave? The police searched there."

"They don't seem to know. The detective said an animal might have carried it there."

I shook my head. "What animal? No animals live in that cave, they wouldn't be able to get in or out, it's too deep, and why would an animal pick up a shoe it had found somewhere else and drop it into the cave?"

Nobody said anything, presumably all three of us were doing the same thing: trying to find some logical explanation, running through various credible or at least imaginable scenarios in our minds, searching for one that might fit.

"Are they going to do anything else?" I asked. "Are they going to examine the cave again?"

Mom shook her head. "I guess it would take more than a shoe for them to reopen the case. If it even is his shoe. And if it is, it doesn't really prove anything."

"It proves that he was there."

"It's almost fifteen years ago," Mom said. She stood up and began to rinse out a cloth under the faucet, mechanically wiped something next to the stove, rinsed out the cloth again.

I didn't know what she meant by saying it was almost fifteen years ago, but I didn't want to ask because I felt as if I ought to know. Maybe she meant it was too late to find anything after so long. Or that the police weren't interested in devoting any more time to the matter. There had been no indication that a crime had taken place, and the fact that someone had found a shoe didn't change that. Or maybe she meant that she couldn't do this anymore. Erik was fifteen when he disappeared, and soon fifteen years would have passed since it happened. They had been without him for almost as long as they had had him.

She was rubbing frantically at the base of the faucet where limescale often formed. Her fingers clutched the dishcloth as if it were something extremely valuable that no one could be allowed to take from her. It provided security, the security of having something to do, because there was always something that needed wiping. There was a security in always appearing to be busy.

She draped the cloth over the faucet.

"I'm going up there," she announced.

"To the mountain?"

She nodded, Dad turned his head away.

"I just want to see it again."

"What's the point?" Dad said quietly.

Mom didn't answer, she was already heading for the hallway.

"I'll come with you," I said quickly.

It was an unconsidered response, and as I put on my shoes and jacket I thought maybe it was a dumb idea, maybe I should have stayed with Dad and let Mom continue to be the unreasonable one, the one who couldn't let go of the knowledge that Erik was gone. And yet I felt it was time. I hadn't been to the mountain since I was a child, when we went there on a class trip. It was fall, we had a picnic at the top and our teacher told us the story of Mount Verity. The deciduous trees in the forest glowed in shades of orange and yellow against a soft gray sky. Some of the boys tried to clamber down into the cave, but were immediately stopped by our teacher, who no doubt pictured someone falling and breaking an arm or a leg. Then we picked mushrooms in the forest down below and identified the different kinds with the help of a set of old guides to fungi. There were no more school trips to the mountain after Erik disappeared.

Now the trees lining the road were fresh and green. The sun was still bright, I felt in my pocket for my sunglasses, thank goodness they were there. We didn't talk in the car. Mom was a worse driver than Dad, more impulsive, and she always drove over the speed limit. There wasn't much traffic, high season for the zoo hadn't kicked in yet, although the parking lot was half full. We continued on to Kvarsebovägen, until Mom turned right onto a narrow track where she parked.

"Is this it?"

She nodded. "I can find my way from here."

We got out of the car and she took a backpack out of the trunk. She locked up, then jumped over the ditch by the side of the track.

"Coming?"

I followed her. I wasn't used to being in the forest at this time of year, the deciduous trees were startlingly green, the day was bright, and the air was fresh. Soon we reached a broad path that immediately began to climb. The tree roots protruding from the ground were gnarled, the sorrel lining the path was as green as the trees and bushes, with its white flowers crowning the leaves. I stopped and plucked a leaf, bit into it, and immediately recognized the fresh, acidic taste. Sorrel used to grow near Erik's and my den in the forest. Sorrel, blueberries, and rock cap fern were like a trinity of treasures, although I never really got the fern, it was hard to clean all the dirt off the roots, and while the sweet taste was okay, I thought the whole thing was kind of pointless, sucking on a fibrous root. I wasn't that desperate for a candy substitute.

Suddenly we were at the top. It really was a beautiful place, we could see for miles, the water sparkled in the spring sunlight and there was a slight mist over Vikbolandet, shading into blue in the distance like in a Renaissance painting. The top of the mountain was rough, the mosses and lichens worn down, it was a popular place for picnics. Someone had arranged large stones in a circle, which was filled with ash and charred wood. A short distance away lay the entrance to the cave, like a wound in the mountain.

Strangely enough, it felt quite ordinary. I had somehow expected more, I had thought about it so many times that it had acquired a mythological status in my mind, grown into something it wasn't, at least not in the late spring's bright sunshine: something terrifying, revolting. I hated this place, but standing there it gave me no reason to.

I thought this couldn't be it, there must be something more—a sign, a logic, a meaning, like the picture in Norrköping's art gallery, I had also thought about that picture many times until it had become like a truth to me, a truth about the truth, which with the passage of time would be revealed to me. As time passes, the truth is revealed and justice follows. But if there was any justice, it wasn't here.

Mom was standing perfectly still, I suddenly noticed the tears running slowly down her cheeks. She looked so small. Small in comparison to the huge mountain, to the background of even higher mountains, to the powerful forest. It was hopeless. All her efforts, which had led to nothing. There was nothing. No grave to visit, nothing to pin her hopes on. Nothing but this cave, this horrible place with its seductive view and portentous history.

Mom slipped off her backpack and put it down on a flat rock, she opened it and took out a flashlight. Then she went over to the cave, switched on the flashlight, and shone the beam down into the darkness, systematically working her way across the rough walls.

"Erik!" she shouted into the cave. "Erik!"

Her voice was small too, small and desperate. Was that how she had sounded all those times when she walked around by herself in the forest, searching? Yelling until she was hoarse, exhausted, yelling to someone who was almost certainly never going to answer. But as long as that wasn't absolutely guaranteed, she kept on trying.

The whole thing was madness. It was madness back then, and it was madness now. Obviously no one was going to answer. But I suddenly felt I couldn't let her shout alone. So I shouted too.

"Erik!" we shouted together, down into the darkness. "Erik!"

It wasn't his shoe. Of course it wasn't his shoe. The police sent pictures for Mom and Dad to identify, and it wasn't that crazy of an idea: an old sneaker of roughly the same brand that Erik used to wear, the rubber was split and dirty, the suede was more or less worn away, but in the pictures where someone had lifted the tongue to reveal the original color you could clearly see that it was green and not blue, plus it was the wrong size.

Dad was angry that evening, a bitter, quiet fury. He called the police incompetent, wondered what idiots they had working on this kind of thing, had they thought we'd look at the shoe and realize the information we'd given them was incorrect? I thought there was something about his anger that had more to do with Mom than with Erik, he was angry because they had reawakened her hope, then immediately taken it away from her. She wandered around the house like a silent shadow, the dishcloth in one hand and a watering can in the other, she wiped the window ledges, nipped off a yellow leaf from a pelargonium, confirmed that nothing needed watering today either.

My brain kept turning everything over when I lay in bed that night, all the old thoughts came back and mingled with the new ones, all the chains of hypotheses and hopes. One thought was that there would somehow be a greater chance of finding one of Erik's shoes now that they'd found one that wasn't his, as if it had somehow increased the odds of finding the right shoe in the forest, which was completely unreasonable because no one knew if there was actually a right shoe to find, and then I thought that the fact there were shoes in the forest was a good sign, kind of like when you're foraging for mushrooms and you find a chanterelle, that means there's a greater chance of finding more than if you don't find any at all, everything going through my brain was idiotic, they were thoughts that might have been reasonable for a twelve-year-old, but that was how I felt as I lay in bed picturing the worn shoe. It was worn in a way that Erik's shoe would have been if such a shoe existed somewhere in the forest, and what would it mean if his shoe actually came back after fifteen years, what would that mean?

Things don't mean as much as you think, a part of my brain informed me, you just imagine stuff, all the connections you think you can see, all the premonitions, all the omens and portents, all the reasons to knock on wood, they are nothing but your imagination. A shoe is just a shoe, it's an object, it has no intentions. And yet in my mind I could see the cave slowly opening up, a shoe was followed by a foot, the mountain slowly restored Erik to the world where he actually belonged, gave him back to us. As if everything had simply been a strange mistake that had now been corrected.

Then I felt ashamed of myself, I was disgusted by the fact that everything in my head was sick and illogical and ridiculous. Such childish, childish thoughts. How childish hope is.

I had been drawing for so long that I had forgotten color existed. I had produced my work by incising the images into copper then printing them on paper, the best-known contemporary faces, just as the old masters would have done: Paris Hilton, Britney Spears, and Jennifer Lopez as if it were the sixteenth century. I did it without too much thought but so skillfully that the Royal Institute of Art finally called me for an interview, at which point I realized I couldn't show up without a story. So I invented one.

It's an artistic style that brings together two traditions, I said, the heritage of the Renaissance and the newer heritage of pop art, it is a dynamic collision between old and new, a meeting between old-fashioned technique and mass production, between Dürer and docusoaps. I want to investigate how we experience time, I said. Contemporary image culture consists largely of instant pictures, transitory paparazzi shots, commercials, a fleeting moment on TV, while a work of art from the Renaissance will last forever. I want to short-circuit our perception of time, I said. I want to find out whether it's possible to freeze our fragmented present to something everlasting.

I knew better than they did that this was what they wanted to hear, so they accepted me. No one asked the perfectly reasonable question—why did I want to give today's most deliberately superficial and commercial cultural expression the weight of something lasting, because no one ever asked questions like that. Art was a lengthy investigation that never needed to present any answers, a process that was never evaluated. Someone said that I was turning Walter Benjamin's idea about the work of art in the age of mechanical reproduction on its head, this was in itself such an impactful idea that nothing more was required, and even though there was more, an interesting feminist aspect to the evaluation of the mass culture that was primarily aimed at female consumers, which in my work I gave the same weight as the male canon we had long regarded as the very definition of art. And then there was my craft, the skill I had developed, my absolute control over the line and the way it was drawn, the small variations in depth and width that made the line thicker and thinner, darker and lighter, I spun a net over the surface of the image that formed a face, a body, a person.

I knew the line as well as I knew myself, and I thought I could see myself in it. A line could be clear, giving definition and contour, but it could also be free and flowing, living and sensual. A simple stroke could express something true and deeply felt. The line had followed me from the Donald Duck comic books and *Starlet* magazines of my childhood, and I had been drawn to work that reminded me of them, to artists who also revered the line: Hokusai, Carl Larsson, Alphonse Mucha, and then Michelangelo's painting, his massive figures where, with the help of the line, he could create such weight and volume that what he painted became more fleshy, more sculptural than many sculptures.

I carried both my story and my paint-stained hands with pride. Graphics destroyed my nails and blackened my hands, I cut my nails as short as possible but still they were never really clean, the greasy, black color ate its way into every crease and crack until my hands looked like printing plates too. It didn't bother me, quite the reverse: my hands were dirty tools that bore witness to my commitment.

From time to time Sylvia came to visit me in my studio. It was always a little awkward, neither of us could really reach the other. We were probably both to blame, but the responsibility was hers. I understood why she had been assigned to me as my advisor, why the department thought she would be able to guide me to my true artistic impression. She had worked on a similar theme but with different techniques, spent the whole of the '90s making video art, sexually explicit films that were regarded as groundbreaking, because the women in them refused to be victims. It was a banal formulation, the simplest possible and yet slightly piquant feminism. She was almost sixty now, still wearing leather pants and heavy boots, lesbian according to my classmates, with an assertive air that made me feel indecisive and uncertain, depressingly prudent with my meticulous drawing. And I assumed that was what she thought of me, she regarded me with a certain amount of contempt that she never really managed to hide.

She sat on an old paint-spattered pine chair that had come with the studio. Sometimes I thought I should throw it away and get a nicer one, but that felt somehow coquettish. There was so much that was unspoken that I had difficulty coming to terms with at the school. Like being surrounded by ugliness. You weren't supposed to care what your studio looked like—either that, or nobody actually did care. In which case that was odd, the idea that people who were studying art, and therefore should have had an appreciation of aesthetics, didn't give a damn what their workplaces looked like, they were full of garbage, empty bottles, unwashed coffee mugs, and everything on the walls had somehow been put up in as ugly a way as possible. I suppose that was an aesthetic of its own, but it wasn't my aesthetic. I had to stop myself from starting to improve my studio, bring in a potted plant, a few rugs, make it into a nice place. Throw out the old pine chair. And yet I felt a sense of tenderness toward it, it was the kind of chair that had been everywhere when I was growing up, and I thought I could see myself in it, rustic and a little bit lost, so it stayed exactly where it was.

As usual Sylvia had wandered around the room, looked at the sketches on my desk, the wall where the finished pages hung from paperclips on the strings I had put up.

"Have you never painted?" she asked.

She always sounded quite stern, although maybe she wasn't, but her whole demeanor made it clear that she wanted honest answers to her questions.

"Only when I had to provide samples to go with my applications for various art schools," I said.

"Didn't you like it?"

"I don't know. I guess I found it difficult. Messy and troublesome. And I'm comfortable with what I'm doing. I've always been good at drawing, so I continued with that."

She nodded. "There was a conflict during the Renaissance, do you know about that?"

I shook my head.

"Between Florence and Venice—*disegno* and *colorito*. Line and color, drawing and painting. It was almost a philosophical issue at the time. Does one achieve the truest image of reality through drawing or painting? In Florence, Michelangelo and Bronzino studied anatomy and produced meticulous drawings, which they then used as the basis of their paintings. And in Venice it was the other way around, Titian and Tintoretto painted directly onto the canvas and built volume with color and light instead of the line. Maybe it's difficult to understand today, but it was a major debate back then among the intellectuals of the day." She paused and smiled at me. "I mean, you don't have to choose. But I've begun to think... Maybe you've taken your expression as far as it can go. It might be useful for you to try something else."

She was right, of course, we both knew that, but it still made me angry. Because I felt caught out, because she had put her finger on something I had thought myself, but hadn't had the strength to tackle. And because the fact that she was right was going to make life difficult: I was going to have to come up with something new and become as good at it as I had become at drawing. How was I going to do that? How was I going to master something in the way that I mastered the line, the line I had been working on ever since I was in school?

"Do you think this is bad?" I asked in a childish attempt to protest, pointing to the wall where my drawings hung in a row, like a celebrity supplement in black and white.

She shook her head.

"Not at all, but how are you going to take it forward? I think it would be good for you to make a clean break and start again with something else."

I thought it was unfair that I wasn't allowed to excel at something. That I had to do something else now that I'd found something I really could do well. Lots of artists did the same thing year in and year out, nobody told them they ought to move their form of expression forward.

When I said that to Sylvia, she laughed.

"Well, maybe someone ought to tell them," she said.

"I just don't know what I'd do instead. I don't know where to go."

"You need to look at your wound," she said firmly. "You need to find your sore point and poke at it."

"My wound? How do you know I have a wound?"

She smiled at me. "Why else would you be in art school? Seriously—we all have a wound, don't we? In fact, we should be happy if we have only one. It's the wounds that make us carry on—because we are carrying something unresolved."

"How can you be sure that this isn't my wound?" I asked, pointing to the wall again.

She shrugged. "Maybe it is? But in that case I still think it could find different forms of expression. I think you should work toward finding the best form for your wound."

I didn't usually trust anyone who wanted to give me advice, and I didn't trust anyone who wanted advice. I always believed that no one knew better than me what it meant to be me, and then I felt ashamed of myself. As if I were so unique. Then again, maybe I was. Maybe everyone was. Maybe the problem was actually contemporary society's obsession with frequently giving good advice. One of the foundation stones of female friendship was the exchange of good advice, all the magazines aimed at girls were built on the premise that women were in need of guidance on everything. Wasn't that actually a declaration that they were incapable of managing alone, easy to capitalize on, measuring their profit in copies sold or friendship involving the exchange of close confidences? Even as a teenager I had thought that it was a sign of weakness in my female friends that they constantly sought advice and affirmation, assurances that the boy they were in love with was definitely interested, that he absolutely had looked at them. The whole thing seemed to me like a kind of game, a demonstrative cementing of loyalty that I found difficult. I couldn't trust anyone if I thought they wanted something from me.

Sylvia was different. Probably because it was very clear that she wasn't giving me advice as part of a transaction. She had nothing to gain, she seemed completely uninterested in me as a person, and not particularly interested in her role as advisor either. No doubt she would rather have been in her own studio devoting her time to her own art.

In addition, she had put her finger on something I had known but had been unwilling to put into words. I was done with graphics. I had exhausted the concept. I had clung to it mainly because everyone else seemed so thrilled with it, even though I knew that wasn't a good reason to continue. I needed Sylvia to say it so that I could fully understand it.

So I bought some oil paints. A set of Becker's normal colors in cool, heavy tubes. I laid them out in color order on the table in my studio and it felt like the first day at school, as if I had lifted the lid of my desk and seen the unused box of crayons lying there like a rainbow smelling of wax, it was the start of something new.

Painting was sensual. Everything was pleasurable, every little detail enjoyable: the resistance when I pressed the brush into the sausage of zinc white on the palette, the consistency of the paint beneath my palette knife as I mixed it to a smooth, single shade. The smells—heavy, thick and oily from the paint, the acrid turpentine, like a concentrated pine forest, like walking through the trees on my way home from visiting Marcus. The whole thing was almost erotic.

I thought I had forgotten everything I'd learned about painting, but the knowledge quickly came back to me. I mixed a cold gray from umber and ultramarine, a warmer tone from Naples yellow and black. As soon as my brush touched the canvas I knew what I had to paint. My gray shades were the color of the mountains, and at the same time I quickly realized that mountains have so many other colors apart from gray, I had to mix new colors, then more new colors for the lichens, they were black, brown, red, and the yellow tending toward ochre, it was rough, rougher than the mountain.

How do you paint something to show that it's rough? To make the mountain look rougher than the water, and the lichen rougher than the mountain? What emerged on my canvas did actually look rough, and I didn't know whether it was because I was able to paint roughness, or if it was the human brain decoding the yellow as rough, based on its experience of the world and the knowledge that lichens are rough. Did the yellow roughness on the canvas really look rough, or was it simply a mutual agreement between the painting and the observer?

It was finding myself in a state far beyond language, where the world turned into signs and symbols, then onto another level that was primal, an intuitive communication of impression and emotion, a state where, by using my colors, I could make someone believe they were looking at something that was rough, or hard, or wet. As if I were creating something absolutely true, a truth about the mountain and the lichen that was a truth about nature itself, that was a truth about life, that was a truth about everything.

And at the same time that truth was merely an illusion, as fragile as a mirage, and it was up to me to maintain it, to become so good at creating the impression of something real that no one could doubt what I painted.

I mixed my paint and I applied it to the canvas and I thought: *Now I'm fooling you. Now I'm fooling you with the truth.*

It had to be perfect. It was an old-fashioned striving, regarded as somewhat suspect. Perfection was seen as dated and inhuman, while anything that showed its flaws was regarded as courageous and human. This was a misconception. In fact the reverse was true: the not-perfect made the artist unreceptive to criticism. It was a defense, a shield to hold up against any objections, which became ineffective if the piece was supposed to be a little ugly, a little careless, a little less than good, if you gave the impression that you didn't care what it looked like.

But if the aim was for it to be perfect, then it had to be perfect. Striving for perfection was to make yourself extremely vulnerable. It was almost like a kind of masochism. I saw perfection before me like Andrea Mantegna's painting of St. Sebastian in the art history book I had read as a teenager: Striving for perfection was like tying your own arms behind you and making yourself a target for the shower of arrows someone is always ready to fire at you. It meant risking everything.

When I was working on graphics, darkness was simply different degrees of black. Now I saw a hundred shades in the darkness, and I painted thick, glowing black, a darkness like newly solidified lava, born out of volcanic fury, still hot beneath my brush. I followed the topography of the mountains like a lover's body, protrusions and hollows, I painted crevices and cavities, water and pine needles, I painted lingon, sphagnum moss, and common haircap, heather like a fleeting violet veil, I painted pine trees and granite, pine trees and granite were my childhood, pine trees and granite were who I was, I painted the delicate loveliness of the early summer, the cow parsley and the nettles. I wanted people to be able to look at my flat stones and rocks and cliffs and see the whole context before them, whole stories: nature rooms, rooms where they themselves had once stood, or could have stood. As if the entire soul of the place could be read in the mountainsides, the coarse gray east coast, chives growing in the cracks, and far away the unbroken horizon, or the pines in the forest on rocky ground, the childhood outings, the sweet smell of mushrooms and rotting leaves in the fall.

Soon I knew the colors as if I had acquired a whole new circle of friends, with qualities and attributes and habits that I had to get to know and accept. Green was fascinating, it was the color that could come across as both the most natural and the most artificial: it could be fresh, lush growth or skies infected by the sulfur from a volcanic eruption, the glowing glasses of absinthe of the Impressionists, the sickly shadow on van Gogh's face. In the same way white was both the purest and the dirtiest color, from the chalky, ceremonial whiteness of antiquity to the grubby garment draped over the shoulder of Caravaggio's Bacchus. Almost nothing that was white was really white: Monet's snow was blue, lilac, pink and apricot, white was both an illusion and a reality, the innocent nakedness of the empty canvas, waiting to be brought to life by being besmirched.

"Have you heard," Sylvia said when she came to visit, "that they found Giotto's skeleton some years ago, beneath one of the churches in Florence? They realized it was him when they analyzed the bones, because they were full of arsenic and lead and copper, all the poisonous substances they used to make paint back in the day."

"As if he had become his own work of art," I said.

She nodded. "As if he had become a part of his own palette."

That seemed absolutely natural to me. The paint had taken possession of me too, led me forward, written its story on the canvases, taught me things I hadn't known before. It made the canvas sing and vibrate, I created surfaces that shimmered, tones that chimed together and formed new entities. Painting meant creating something completely new and something ancient at the same time. It made me go into myself, follow a path leading deeper and farther back until it felt as if I had found something in there that was significantly older than me. I was in contact with something primeval, something archaic lurking down there, and it was painting that made the connection.

I poked at it with my brush, I wanted and didn't want to wake it from its slumber, but when it moved, deep down inside me in the darkness, I wanted nothing more than to continue poking at it, like a mosquito bite I couldn't stop scratching.

It was bigger than anything I had encountered previously in life, a simultaneously peaceful and violent force, and it felt as if I were a part of something eternal, something that had gone on for millennia, something that others had poked at just like I was doing, from those who painted horses and oxen on cave walls right up to today, as if I were linked to all those before me who had felt what I was feeling, my fears were the fears of the whole of humanity, my sorrow was the same as all previous sorrows, my darkness was a part of an endless darkness.

I painted my way down into the abyss, and when I reached the bottom all I wanted to do was to stay there.

I gave up almost everything I used to do. I stopped running and I stopped socializing. Not that I'd had many people to hang out with, but we saw one another in class from time to time, someone was throwing a party or we went out somewhere. All of that suddenly seemed meaningless, I just thought it was a waste of energy. It was hard not to drink when everyone else was drinking, and I always had more fun when I was drunk, but I hated the hangover the following day. If my brain wasn't sharp and clear I couldn't get anything of value done, and lying in bed feeling tired and nauseous, knowing that the day was wasted, stressed me out and gave me a crawling sense of anxiety that couldn't be chased away with anything but work. From thinking that no day counted for very much, I was now filled with the belief that every day was vitally important, every hour. Every hour was an hour of life, an hour when I could achieve something that wouldn't have been achieved if I hadn't done it, that wouldn't have existed in a world without me. That realization was more intoxicating than alcohol.

I got up early in the mornings and walked to my studio, from the small apartment at Södra station, along Swedenborgsgatan down to Hornsgatan, on to Slussen, Skeppsbron, Blasieholmen, the air was filled with the smells of moving water, exhaust fumes, and freshly baked bread, the boats shuttled back and forth on Stockholm's river.

The concept of the sea was better than the actual sea, I had thought every time I was on a boat. The concept of love was better than love, I had thought every time I was in a relationship. But the concept of art was not better than art. Art itself was superior to all concepts surrounding it. It came before the thought, it was sufficient in itself. I wished I had been able to think the same about love, but I couldn't. That was just the way it was.

I was often the first to arrive at the school, I had to switch off the alarm, turn on the lights, and put the coffee on. Then I would pick up from where I had finished the previous day, I would paint until lunchtime, eat something simple in my studio, crispbread, tuna, egg, continue painting until the day was over and it was time to go home again. It was as if time had been paused, everything around me disappeared. Even I myself disappeared. It was like when I was waking up in the mornings and for a moment I didn't know whether it was summer or winter, whether I was lying in my childhood bed or next to someone I loved, whether I actually loved the person I was lying next to, everything was still unknown, everything was fluid. Who are we really? Who are we in that state, who are we under normal circumstances?

Painting allowed me, for a while, to stop being me. What a blessing to stop being me.

During our final exhibition I was already represented by a gallery. I exhibited three paintings, a triptych of large canvases I had worked on for the whole of my final year. The largest, in the center, featured a mountain with an opening, a dark entrance. The motif continued over the two flanking canvases, where the trunks of the pine trees stood tall and straight, like columns of some unknown order carrying a joist that was outside the scope of the image. It was twilight, further back in the picture the forest was already dark.

The word "grotto" is a loan word from the Italian, where it means the same thing, and the Italian *grotta* comes from *grupta* in medieval Latin, which in turn comes from *crupta* in classical Latin. "Crypt" and "grotto" were the same word initially, before history divided it in two. Art originated in caves, where the first human beings painted horses and oxen and made handprints. The early Christian icon painters worked in the crypts of Rome's catacombs. They painted their pictures on the walls, pictures that were not allowed to exist up in the light, pictures of something true, something greater than themselves, which would form the first links in a chain leading to all those who shared their belief moving forward through history. There is something in the cave that is connected to the very origins of art, with the dark and mystical quality that once was a self-evident part of it, but we have increasingly distanced ourselves from that quality by dragging art into white rooms and demanding that it tell us about contemporary society, take social responsibility, become a kind of letter of indulgence that will buy us a clear conscience. All of this is a million miles away from the original function of art. Maybe it would be better for us to move back toward the cave. Maybe that would be better for art.

Richard Sandberg, who owned the gallery where I was to exhibit, had listened attentively to everything

I said. He was handsome in an upper-class way, well-dressed, and he was regarded as young even though he must have been about forty. The fact that he exhibited several of the major established Swedish artists while at the same time having the courage to take a chance on some of the new ones gave the Sandberg Gallery a youthful, avant-garde profile in spite of the fact that it was in Östermalm.

"You can imagine," he said, waving his hand at the central canvas on the wall, "that those tree trunks really are columns. And that they are holding up the roof of a temple we can't see. That nature, so to speak... is a sacred place."

Of course you could imagine that. I had thought it was obvious, but he seemed to believe he was very clever to have worked it out on his own, which was a good thing as far as I was concerned, so I nodded.

I insisted that my paintings from the final exhibition were not three separate works but one single piece, and although it was difficult to sell something so large, Richard did exactly that—to a private collector who was building up an extensive collection of contemporary art. The sale was talked about within the art world, the fact that someone had paid so much for the work of an unestablished artist, which meant that I began to be regarded as a rising star.

Just over a year later I had my first solo exhibition at Richard's gallery, I painted with equal concentration leading up to it, I was totally absorbed, and for the first time in years I felt free. I stretched my canvases and stood in front of them, full of confidence. I rented a studio in a manor house in Hornstull thanks to Sylvia, who had known the previous tenant, an elderly artist who had been forced to give up the lease when age prevented him from continuing to paint. The floor was stained with paint that had probably been there since the '70s, the bathroom and the tiny kitchen bore no resemblance to all those realtor's brochures that tried to depict Hornstull as fresh and hip, a leftover of an unrenovated Stockholm that was rapidly disappearing, but I liked it despite that—or perhaps because of it. And at the exhibition all of my paintings sold, most during the private view.

Richard produced a slim catalogue, I asked Sylvia to write the text.

To speak of art in terms of "an investigation" has become something of a cliché these days. This often turns out to be a method of camouflaging the fact that it is actually the opposite: a portrayal of convictions that were already established within the artist long before the artistic process began—and which then simply fulfill the function of a receptacle for those convictions.

However, in Hanna Hallman's work we really do get the impression that an investigation is going on.

An investigation of what?

The mountains appear mute, almost dismissive. They are eternal, for good or evil: they connect us to an age so long before us that it is hard to imagine. And yet they are, compared with a human being's short time on this earth, constant, immovable. Everything else around us changes during a lifetime—cities look different as buildings are torn down and erected. Nature changes character, both because we fell forests and use up the earth's resources, but also because of those forces that exist within nature itself. One species takes over at the cost of another, the landscape of our childhood is suddenly overgrown and dark or ravaged and bare, affected by storms, wildfires, and floods.

But the mountains remain intact.

If we choose to regard them from a longer time perspective, another picture emerges. The Earth's continents were once joined together. Parts of the world that are distant from one another today used to be connected, united by the mountains, and maybe one day they will be again: the continental drift is not over, but something that is ongoing. The same applies to the mountains. Extremely slow geographical processes expose them to changes that a human being finds it difficult to perceive, but these processes are very real. Pressure, movement, and chemical alterations mean that the mountain is altered, that one type of mountain can become another. The mountains, like art, seem to suspend time.

Hanna Hallman's painting can be described as both naive and realistic. It is a mixture of the child's magical ideas and science's professed objectivity, simultaneously romantic and matter-of-fact. Her mountains sometimes seem to verge on the human: the granite could be flesh, the grass could be hair, every patch and crevice could be a patch and crack in the fragile skin that holds a human being together. The mountain is both an object for our fantasies and almost an independent organism: we look at it and think that it could have agency, a consciousness, an intention. That the mountain could in some sense be alive.

The mountains have been central to Hallman's art over the past five years. For five years she has focused all of her interest on the very foundations beneath our feet, approached them with the close attention a person in love dedicates to the object of their desire, or a police officer applies to a crime scene.

What is it that she hopes will be revealed in this investigation?

I don't think I am on the wrong track if I answer: The truth.

III

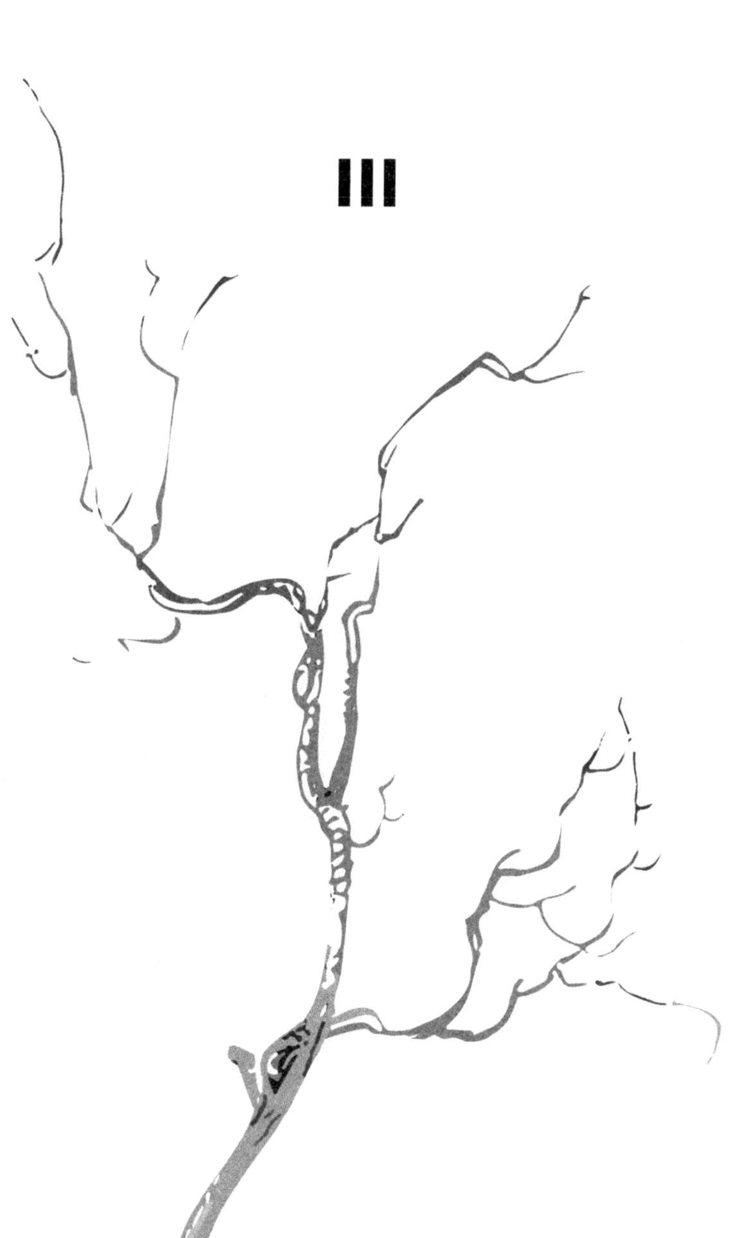

When the train finally leaves the platform we have been sitting on it for almost half an hour. The delay has been caused by a staff changeover, according to an announcement over the loudspeaker. It is warm on board, even though we are sitting on the side that is in the shade. Nicholas has already drunk more than half the water. When he notices that the train is moving, he beams and gives me a thumbs up. He is very patient as long as he has something to do, and to be on the safe side I bought a coloring book and a packet of candy at Central Station, but so far he has been happy with his iPad. The theme song to *Paw Patrol* seeps out through his headphones.

I always think that the journey out of Stockholm feels symbolic, as if the city were shaped on the basis of a pedagogical idea: the inner city ends at the Årsta Bridge with its lovely view of the city and the water, then you are immediately on the outskirts, among the marshaling yards, warehouses, suburbs, then Södertälje, then the countryside. It is like being transported through a color plate in a children's book about how the city is constructed.

Mom and Dad pick us up at the station, they didn't need to do that, it's only a ten-minute walk and we don't have much luggage. But there they are, smiling and suntanned.

Nicholas runs on ahead and gives them a big hug. They hug me too when I reach them, ask if everything went okay.

"It was fine once we got away," I reply.

"It's lucky you weren't due to come yesterday," Dad says. "There was an electrical fault, and nothing moved for several hours."

"There's always something," Mom adds.

They never travel by train, but they obviously keep themselves informed, presumably through the radio, P4 is on in the kitchen all day every day, just like when I was little. When I was a teenager I used to change the station as soon as I was alone, anything was better than P4, with its depressing old tunes that were played to death.

Dad loads our cases into the trunk and we get in the car. It's warm in there too, warmer than on the train.

"I'm too hot!" Nicholas says. "Put the fan on!"

"It'll be better once we start moving," I reassure him. "And we're not going far, it will only take a few minutes."

It's not long since we last drove from the center to the house, yet it seems to me as if everything has changed a little. They've repainted the waterworks down by the stream in a lurid shade of apricot, and there's something different about the play area, maybe they've put up new swings.

"Can we go there?" Nicholas asks, pointing.

"Absolutely—but we're going to have lunch first."

"It's only herring with potatoes," Mom says. "But I thought it might be suitable in this hot weather."

"It'll be perfect," I assure her.

The street isn't much different either, apart from a few small developments: someone's hedge has grown tall and dense, one of the properties on the hill has new wooden decking. Dad drives slowly, there isn't much room between all the "Beware—children playing" signs.

"The Ekmans have bought a trampoline for their grandchildren," he informs us. "They said you're welcome to go over there if Nicholas wants to give it a try."

"Can we?" Nicholas says eagerly.

"Of course, but maybe not today."

"Why not?"

"We're going to be here for several days, we've got plenty of time. You said you wanted to go to the play area."

And here we are. The house is exactly the same. The coolness of the hallway, the rattle of the beaded curtain. The smell of home, wood and slightly stuffy air. Copies of the local paper, *Norrköpings Tidning*, piled up on the bench in the kitchen, nectarines in Grandma's old bowl, a kind of deep silence that cannot be chased away by the enthusiastic voices on the radio.

"When are we eating?" Nicholas wants to know.

"In a little while," Dad says. "Would you like a nectarine in the meantime?"

Nicholas goes out through the back door clutching the nectarine, I watch him disappear into the shade of the big cherry tree, where the shed housing the outdoor toys is located.

The potatoes have already been peeled and are in the pan, so there isn't much I can do to help. I offer to set the table, but Dad tells me that has already been taken care of too, he points through the window to the seating area out front. The generous parasol is up to protect us from the sun.

"Are many of the neighbors on vacation?" I ask when the food is ready and we are seated at the table. "It's so quiet here."

"The Norrgårds have gone to their summer cottage and the Larssons are in Denmark," Dad says. "I don't think Anna and Gösta are home either, but I don't know where they've gone. Maybe to Halmstad."

I nod, eat my herring. This is the kind of conversation adults had when I was a child, and now that I'm having it, I can see from Nicholas's expression that he thinks it's just as boring as I used to think back then. I don't find it particularly interesting either, but at least it's a conversation.

There is so much we've never talked about. Like Erik's disappearance and how it affected all of us, what it did to us as a family. What it did to me. Or what we really think happened to him. Whether Mom and Dad still hope, somewhere deep down, that he will come back. There seems to be a tacit agreement that we will never bring it up, never mention Erik except in passing. I suppose it's a way of being able to go on living, I sometimes think. No better or worse than other ways. But occasionally it feels as if our conversations are a permanent evasion of what really matters, because it would be too painful.

We haven't discussed my separation from John either, or the reasons behind it. I have said a couple of things about how Nicholas reacted (better than we could have hoped, after a brief period of separation anxiety and difficulty getting to sleep at night), but it has all been very discreet, tiptoeing around the subject. Not that I would have wanted it any other way. If we had been a different kind of family I can imagine us talking about everything. Going over and over what had happened, analyzing, delving into events, feelings, relationships. Like in a movie about the middle classes, where every dinner ends with someone wanting to talk things out. We never talk things out, we try to have a pleasant time. We know that our lives are so different from one another's that it would be foolish to make that fissure any bigger: it is better to try to hold together what is possible.

My parents rarely say anything about my art. I know they are proud of me, but maybe also uncomfortable. Of course they realize that everything I do is about Erik. Perhaps they feel I am exploiting something private, a grief that also belongs to them. Perhaps they simply don't want to be reminded.

After lunch Nicholas drags me into the backyard, where he has set out the croquet hoops. We only manage to hit a few balls before he starts saying he wants to go to the play area, so I give in and take him by the hand. Together we go down the hill, the same route I walked every day on my way to elementary school, then I cycled for six years to junior high, then three more years on my way to catch the bus into town and my high school. How many times have I traveled along this road? I try to work it out, get to two thousand four hundred at a conservative estimate, I went this way before I started school too, I walked and cycled along here on my way to visit friends or to go shopping. Three thousand times? Probably more. Four thousand? It's hardly surprising that I still remember it so clearly. The thick cypress hedge at the first house on the left, on the other side of the street the lamppost and the electricity box, both in matte gray galvanized steel, behind them another hedge, one with small oval red berries and sharp thorns, I cycled into it once, the asphalt was broken up beside the verge, the ground was sandy, with hare's-foot clover and lupins growing in it. Someone has cleared away the lupins, they are regarded as invasive and dangerous these days.

This deep familiarity with the landscape of my childhood, which isn't even a landscape but roadside verges in a residential area, is a knowledge that has no value whatsoever, yet at the same time it is everything in a way, a kind of foundation within a human being, anchoring them in the world.

The play area is in a hollow, surrounded by a lawn that seemed gigantic to me when I was a child. There is a soccer field next door, in the winter the road-cleaning service sprayed it with water and we skated in the glow of the streetlamps, that is a clear memory, razor-sharp in my mind: the hard piles of snow around the edges of the ice, the dark, starlit sky up above.

But now it is summer, and I am an adult. The parents of those who were children back then are retirees now, and those who were children are the new adults. And so it will continue. As I contemplate the new swings in the play area, maybe someone in the next generation will contemplate another set of new swings. The ones that were there were already looking scruffy in the '80s, I remember the flaking paint on the green posts, you could pull it off in fragile pieces that were rusty on the back.

The new posts are made of wood, the whole thing feels very solid, but I still have to tell Nicholas to be careful when he swings high and with enthusiasm, a terrifying image comes into my mind, one of the chains comes loose from its fixing and he flies through the air, lands headfirst on the sand.

I am tired, I got up early to pack. Even if we're not staying long, there is always a lot to bring, swimming trunks and toys and sunscreen and comics and cables and chargers, and then my own stuff, which I always pack last, underwear, my makeup bag, a novel I know I'm not going to read.

I sit down on a bench that is also new, the old one was pale yellow, painted in a thick layer of plasticized paint, this one is tastefully lasered in gray. My childminder used to sit on the yellow bench when I was little and we came here, sometimes she would smoke a cigarette. No one does that these days, especially not childminders, if there actually are any childminders anymore. Anyway, no one is smoking, and there are no lupins that might spread and lay waste to the entire community. Little by little, the world is being rearranged.

I take out my phone. Richard has emailed, he emails a lot. I've always thought I had an unnecessarily well-developed need for control, but that was before I met him. His tone is always pleasant, almost over the top, yet at the same time demanding. This time he is wondering if there are any changes to the list of works, he has started to plan the exhibition that is due to open at the end of September. It is July. The distance between July and September feels immense, but of course it isn't. Just over two months. Maybe it's normal to start planning at this stage. I don't know, I've never had such a big exhibition before. My own exhibition at Liljevalchs gallery. They are going to print a poster showing some of my paintings, to be displayed all over Stockholm. We need to choose which pieces will go on the poster too. And we need to decide on a title for the exhibition. There is a lot to do. To be honest not all the paintings are finished yet, maybe some of them haven't actually been started, but I daren't tell Richard that.

I'm not working at the moment, I reply. *I'll be back in the studio next week, will contact you then.*

It is a sadistic response to someone like him, he will fret all week, but in this place it is impossible to think about my paintings. I have never been able to work at my parents' house, it is a different world, a world that has nothing to do with that other world, my work in the studio, yet of course it has everything to do with it. But I cannot be an artist when I am with Mom and Dad. I am an artist in Stockholm.

Nicholas is clattering around on a jungle gym that leads to the slide, when he gets right to the top he smiles and waves to me. He is so like John when he smiles. I thought John was incredibly good-looking when we met. I still thought so when we broke up, but by then the electricity between us had gone, I could see with the distance of familiarity that he was good-looking from a purely objective standpoint, but it no longer affected me.

We met when I was having my paintings framed for one of the exhibitions at the gallery. Richard had worked with him for years, and entrusted a lot of the framing to him. According to Richard, John is the only frame-maker in the city who understands anything about art. I went with him to a large, messy workshop in Liljeholmen, a former industrial building. Richard and his assistant carried one of the large canvases together, and John, who was standing cutting passe-partout frames when we arrived, put down his scalpel to help out, he gently placed my painting on the large table and said it was fantastic.

"Are you the painter?" he asked.

"I am," I said, embarrassingly self-conscious all of a sudden.

"Fantastic," he said again.

I knew right away that I wanted something to happen. To go to bed with him initially, the attraction was instant, the image of him silhouetted against the large windows in the workshop etched itself onto my brain. Maybe he experienced something similar, because only a few days later he messaged me to ask if I could come by to check something out. I went over that same afternoon.

"To be perfectly honest, I just wanted to see you again," he said when I got there, he looked at me in a way that made me go weak at the knees in the beginning, his gaze was steady, direct, honest. I thought it was the most wonderful thing anyone had ever said to me.

We drank coffee on the loading bay, it was April, dusty spring, sunshine that appeared kind of faded. He told me he had also gone to Galleri Mejan, part of the Royal Institute of Art, a few years before me, but had given up art and become a frame-maker instead.

"I was always a better craftsman than an artist," he said.

"I feel the same," I replied.

He shook his head. "You're equally good at both. Like everyone wishes they were."

We talked all afternoon. Then we strolled together across Liljeholmen Bridge and up Hornsgatan, where the grit leftover from winter had recently been swept away, the whole street looked new and the twilight was endless, the sky was pink for several hours. We went into a bar and had a few drinks, got just drunk enough for me to pluck up the courage to ask if he wanted to come home with me for a nightcap, and he did.

Was it love? I don't know. When the first attraction had faded, it quickly turned into something else. I wanted a child, I wanted what other people had. Security. Someone to share everything with, someone to hold me and tell me that everything would be all right.

He soon stopped holding me, but everything was all right anyway: I had a child, a son. I knew I would have a son, it almost felt as if I had ordered him, or at least wished for him with such intensity that God or fate or whoever makes these decisions had been unable to miss it, and had agreed to give me what I wanted.

I had thought that I couldn't have children. I had gotten pregnant several times when I was younger, but had always had an early miscarriage, it simply slipped out of me as if it couldn't find anything to hold on to in there, and in the end I had stopped using protection. When John and I met I was pregnant after three weeks and when I continued being pregnant I thought it was meant to be. As if nature had a plan.

We had only known each other for a week or so when he asked if I would like to see his boat. It was a wooden vessel that was out of the water on the island of Långholmen, it was old and had been in a poor state when he bought it, he had renovated it himself. When I climbed on board I understood what he'd meant when he said he was a craftsman rather than an artist. The frames he made might have been the best in Sweden, but they seemed simple in comparison with the boat. In addition to all the exterior parts he had improved and maintained, he had made new solutions for interior storage, shelves with smooth edges, cupboards with a special kind of latch that stopped them from flying open in rough seas, teak frames on springs so that you could tuck things behind them, leather straps to secure other things with. It was all so meticulously done that it looked like an organic continuation of the hull, as if the shelves and cupboards had slowly grown out of the body of the boat itself.

A month or so later the boat was in the water and I was invited for a trip. It was late spring, the air was still cold even though the sun was shining, it was reflected in the water that lay before us like a silvery mirror. There was a light breeze coming straight toward us, so we had to yaw from side to side, John was delighted. That was when I realized how different we were. I would have preferred a calm, peaceful outing, moving along with a gentle following wind. John wanted to sail for real, he saw it as a meaningful activity and not simply a way of transporting oneself, like another craft that he had mastered.

"Isn't this great?" he said.

He was so much more enthusiastic than me, in every aspect of his character. Next to him I felt slow and boring, bad-tempered and negative. My feeling that the concept of the sea was better than the sea itself wouldn't go down well with him. So I nodded.

"Absolutely."

I was in the early stages of pregnancy. Tired and nauseous, almost as if I were sleepwalking, possibly paralyzed by my hormones as well as the realization that I was pregnant, that every hour I stayed pregnant was an hour closer to what was growing inside me emerging as a child rather than a blood clot.

John wasn't wearing a lifejacket. I had borrowed one, a sun-bleached orange Helly Hansen, which must have been old and had probably lost most of its ability to float. I decided I would buy a new one for the next time.

"Why aren't you wearing a lifejacket?" I asked.

He shrugged. There was no good answer, he just didn't wear one. He had been taught to sail by his grandfather, who didn't bother with a lifejacket either. Plus he was a good swimmer.

"But it must be a long time since you learned to sail?" I said. "In the '80s? Maybe they didn't wear lifejackets back then. Just like they didn't always wear seatbelts in the car. People didn't think anything was dangerous in those days. But what if the boom hit you on the head? Being a good swimmer won't help if you're unconscious."

The boom made me nervous. I understood that John could predict its movements, but I also knew that it could do whatever it wanted if the winds were capricious, you could never be sure it wouldn't swing around with speed and force.

So I bought myself a new lifejacket and a thin buoyancy vest for John, which he reluctantly agreed to use. I was certain he wouldn't wear it when he was alone, a childish expression of doing what he wanted. *I'm never letting our child be alone with him in the boat*, I thought at the time, before there was any guarantee that we would have a child.

We were sitting in the cockpit one evening that summer, when it was warmer and we could sleep on board. I was still pregnant, less tired but no less anxious, and no less uncomfortable with spending time on a boat. John had brought beer, alcohol-free for me, and we drank it as the sun went down. He had tipped a packet of salted peanuts into a plastic glass, and was eating them by grabbing a fistful and throwing them into his mouth.

"Please don't do that," I said eventually. "What if you get one stuck in your throat?"

"That's never happened," he replied.

"Knock on wood," I said, knocking on wood. The entire boat was made of wood, so it was easy. I opted for the table.

A man who was going to be the father of my child had to be careful, I thought. He mustn't take any stupid risks. He couldn't disappear.

And then we had a child. He was born in the most boring, most long-drawn-out winter, and the whole thing seemed incomprehensible to me, the idea that he had been inside me for all those months, and he had grown from a tiny seed into a complete person. At first his gaze was dark and inscrutable, as if he were actually very old, not new to the world at all. It was as if time short-circuited when my eyes met his, I felt as if he were looking back at me from the dawn of time, as if my womb were a dark cave from which he had finally broken out, and all the smells that surrounded us in those early days confirmed my suspicions: smells of iron and earth, the fluid that continued to trickle out of me could have come from underground, filtered through rocks and minerals, mud and sediment from a primeval age. Nothing in my experience of having a child had any connection to the pastel-colored blankets and soft little hats that were suddenly all around us, I regarded them as civilization's clumsy attempts to hide what was really going on: something dark and violent, something frightening, archaic.

I found the baby years difficult, with their sticky physicality, like the memory of the dolls' corner at the church children's group, a world built for a different kind of woman than me. John wasn't interested in family life, maybe I wasn't either. Even when I had a family of my own I never stopped thinking that there was something dutiful about it all, something that didn't suit me. I had never liked the idea of becoming absorbed into a "we," because "we" inevitably meant waiving a part of myself. Not that my self was huge and needed space, rather the reverse: my self was so small that I couldn't afford to waive any part of it, I wanted to hang on to the little that there was, for myself and for my art, and when I had a child he too needed a part of me, he had to have as much as I could possibly give him, and that was the end of me, and the end of the "we" too.

I had a feeling that John was surprised to find that I didn't make a huge effort: he seemed to be used to coming and going as he pleased, keeping his self exactly as it had always been and letting the other half of the "we" be the one who made sure the constellation worked. But since I wasn't that kind of person, neither of us made an effort to hold it together, and in the end there was nothing left and we split up. At least then I could stop waiting for life to begin, because in many ways it already had: suddenly I was over forty, separated, I had Nicholas every other week, I was able to make a living as an artist.

There were still boxes that we hadn't unpacked when we split up. *Very practical,* I thought cynically, we didn't need to pack everything away again. Nicholas was so little that he soon forgot that there was a time when all three of us lived together. But John was still the only frame-maker in the city who knew anything about art, so he was going to make the frames for my exhibition in the fall. We were linked to each other for the rest of our lives, through Nicholas and the frames.

But now it is summer and Nicholas is tired of the play area. We chase each other for a while on the big lawn until we are both out of breath, then we set off for home. I point out a bush between the street and a yellow brick house.

"Huckleberries grow here in the fall," I said.

This is a meaningless piece of information as far as he is concerned. I have shown him the white berries in Stockholm, but he wasn't impressed. His attitude toward them is nowhere near what mine was at his age, which I found slightly disappointing. The fact that I couldn't share the joy of the berries known as firecrackers with my child.

"Erik and I used to make them explode on the way to school," I say.

"Okay."

"We came along here every day. We were usually together in the mornings, but not in the afternoons. He finished later than me because he was older."

"Okay," Nicholas says again.

To him Erik is merely a story, a mythological figure he has heard about all his life, but has no relationship with, no image apart from the photographs that are still around. The first ones are a kind of murky brown, the way photos were in the '70s and early '80s, and the last ones are illuminated by a cold flash, as if the development of camera technology followed the fashion, or maybe it was the other way around. Erik starts off with a blond pageboy cut, then his hair is short and a little spiky, a typical '80s style, nothing fancy, that was just how boys looked at the time. In one of the murky brown pictures he is sitting on the old sofa in the living room with me on his lap. I am only a baby, my face is red and strangely distorted, while Erik must be about four years old and looks cute and positively cherubic: round cheeks, blond hair the color of honey. Behind us seagrass wallpaper, the leaves of a Swiss cheese plant. I have taken a picture of the photo with my phone, and I look at it sometimes. Of course I have no memory of the occasion when someone, presumably Dad, took it, and Erik probably wouldn't have remembered either, perhaps nobody does; it was most likely a Saturday or Sunday, because Erik is smartly dressed as if we had guests. I presume it was the winter of 1979, it is so long ago. A day that no one remembers anymore.

"To think that the bush is still here," I say, distractedly touching a branch. "It must be at least forty years old. Maybe fifty."

Nicholas has stopped listening, he has found a stick by the roadside and is swishing it through the air.

"Are you hungry?" I ask. "Shall we fix a snack when we get home?"

There is no need, because Mom has heated up pastries from the freezer and mixed a pitcher of juice, with ice cubes that clink when she pours it. We eat in the backyard, Nicholas and Dad shuttle back and forth between the table and the croquet lawn, laughing and shouting. Nicholas is barefoot, with a pastry clutched in his hand, he looks happy. It makes me feel ashamed, because this is how I think a child ought to grow up. The way I did, in a house with a garden where you can play croquet and race in and out, barefoot, create your own little world in the backyard, and as you grow up you gradually explore farther afield.

Erik and I built dens in the forest, I was still very young then, I don't think I'd even started school. At some point he started to feel that playing with his kid sister was childish, but from time to time he gave in. He was good at building dens, he had the technical skills. I was better at the aesthetics even then, I made them look nice. Swept the needles from the floor with a broom made from pine branches.

Nicholas has never built a den in the forest. What a poor upbringing. He has been to various play areas in Södermalm, stood in line for the swings in his Polarn O. Pyret fleece among children with weird names. I have often thought that we ought to move to Kolmården. Buy a big old house where I could use one of the rooms as a studio. But it's out of the question. John is in Stockholm, and even if he isn't interested in family life, he is a good dad, a devoted dad. He and Nicholas have fun together, it often seems as if they have more fun than Nicholas and me. John would never allow me to have Nicholas more than he does, and he definitely wouldn't let us move away. And it is good for me to be in Stockholm. It is so easy to lose touch with the art world if you're not in close proximity to it. During the weeks when Nicholas is with John I make a point of going to private viewings and exhibitions, not only to see them but to be seen. You have to be seen, you have to be on people's radar so that they will remember you next time they want a guest tutor or to order a public work of art. That's how you continue to be someone within the art world.

"I was thinking of starting to go through the closets later," I say to Mom.

"There's no hurry. It's so hot."

The neighbor's cat pokes his head around the side of the shed.

"Hansson!" Mom calls to him. "Come on, Hansson!"

It's an unusual name for a cat, but it suits him. With his compact body and slightly strutting gait, he somehow resembles an elderly gentleman.

"Nicholas! Look who's here!"

We play with the cat for a while until Nicholas makes a sudden movement, and Hansson scurries off into the shade beneath the cherry tree.

Mom and Dad are probably going to sell the house. They haven't quite made up their minds yet, at least that's what they say, but they are leaning in that direction. They can't see any reason to hang on to it, except for Nicholas's sake—they agree with me that a child should have the chance to run around barefoot on a lawn, but we don't come to visit very often. We should make more of an effort. If they decide not to sell, we will.

They have started to view apartments in Norrköping. With the money they would get for the house they would be able to afford a large apartment in a beautiful old building, right in the center of town. That would enable them to enjoy things they have begun to appreciate, but rarely do: eat out, go to the theater or a concert.

They never did anything like that when Erik and I were growing up, people just didn't do that back then, I can't remember ever hearing that someone's parents had gone to the theater. But they have started to do it now.

I've often wondered why they didn't move years ago. At first they stayed for my sake, I get that. They didn't want to tear me away from a familiar environment. It would have been easier for them to leave Kolmården, to escape from a place where everything reminded them of Erik. Where his room was exactly as he left it, that's how it was for many years until they finally removed his possessions. At the time it didn't occur to me how painful that must have been. The final admission that he wasn't coming back. That he would never play any more records on his stereo, would never spend another night in his bed.

And the whole area was a reminder of what had happened. It was impossible to drive past the church without thinking that this was the last place he had been before the boys set off for the mountain, impossible to drive east toward the zoo without thinking that this was the last route he had cycled, impossible to think about Mount Verity and its stories without everything flooding back. Mom and Dad must have done everything they could to avoid having to go in that direction. We never went to the zoo together after Erik disappeared, the only times I visited were with the school or a friend's family.

And people must have looked at them, talked about them. If they had moved they would have been able to start afresh, in a new house where Erik had never lived, in a new place where no one knew them, where the tragedy they had experienced didn't provide fuel for speculation and new stories, new myths told in whispering voices to the children of new generations. But they stayed, and they did it for my sake, and maybe out of a kind of defiance, a protest against circumstances over which they had no control. Staying was their decision, a decision they could stick to, as if they were asserting their rights against fate, unhappiness, death. The Mountain.

Time helped. The fact that it continued to pass was the only thing that gave them hope. Time is a double-edged sword. It can console, and it can instill fear. I often want it to stop. I often think that I want to fight against time, subdue it, lock it down in this exact situation, where my son is still a child and my parents are still fit and healthy, because soon all that will change. The only thing we know for sure about time is that things will change.

But now is now. Now it is summer and I am standing in my old bedroom, and the inside of my closet doors are covered in posters, stuck on with Blu-Tack that has grown old and made greasy marks in the corners, Brett Anderson, Jarvis Cocker, a black-and-white postcard of a llama looking out of a New York cab.

The first closet is full of stuff, old sketch pads and loose drawings, a box of hair scrunchies and bobbles, dried-up nail polish and half-empty perfume bottles where the contents have gone cloudy, boxes of letters from former pen pals, a pile of *VeckoRevyn* magazines, a bundle of school yearbooks. The other closet contains the records and cassette tapes I didn't take with me when I left home, I can't even bring myself to open it.

It all feels so overwhelming. And slightly disgusting. Maybe I should just throw the whole lot away. When am I ever going to need any of this again? Apart from the school yearbooks—I should probably keep them. I open one, from the last year of elementary school. In our class photo, Marcus and I are standing in the back row. He is dressed in black, staring straight into the camera with a serious expression. My bangs are too short and I am wearing a gray sweater, I look uncomfortable, almost as if I want to apologize for being in the picture, taking up space, existing in the world. I look sad. *How lucky I was that Marcus liked me,* I thought. *How lucky that some of his self-confidence rubbed off on me.*

I close the book and put it back in the box. I'm not going to be able to tackle this right now. Instead I go into Erik's old room. It is a guest room and hobby room now, there is a sewing machine on a table by the window and the sofa is a sofa bed. And yet it is as if something of Erik still lingers. Perhaps it is because of the light, the sparkling patches of sunlight filtering in through the leaves of the tall birch tree outside the window, it's just like it used to be.

I remember the coverlet on Erik's bed, a soft, velvety fabric, with stripes of white and different shades of green. It was nice to lie on, even if I didn't do it very often, but I remember a few times when he was sitting at his bulky pine desk working on something: for a while he painted tiny soldiers that I think were supposed to represent those who fought in the American Civil War. He didn't really take much notice of me, I lay on his bed like a pet, a cat, contented simply to be near him, as younger siblings are: grateful, submissive.

It's strange how close siblings are. I have memories of him that are so intimate it's almost embarrassing: the smell of his sweaty feet, the sharpness of his elbows when he poked me if we fell out. We were never really close, we didn't confide in each other, and yet there was an intimacy between us, a biological, almost animal intimacy that linked us together. Standing here in his room I still think I can smell him, and that smell is also a part of me.

He once gave me a car for my Barbie dolls as a Christmas present. A pink sports car, it must have been expensive, but he had earned money selling Christmas magazines, and maybe he was still young enough not to understand the value of money. Or else he really wanted to give me something special. I was thrilled. Thrilled and a little ashamed because I had given him something cheap and not particularly nice, he was difficult to buy presents for. The Barbie car was my best present that year. Until then my Barbie dolls had had to make do with Mom's high-heeled shoes as a substitute car, but now the door was open to new, more realistic games, and my friends came over between Christmas and New Year's and we built a garage out of a shoebox and had

Barbie and Ken drive to the beach, where they had sex behind a spider plant that we borrowed from the living room.

I open one of the closets. Mom and Dad are using it to store stuff that they don't have room for anywhere else: a few rolled-up canvases, a row of folders with blue spines. They have kept some of Erik's things too, on one of the shelves are old boxes of Lego sets. The picture on the top one shows a cheerful Lego man in a space suit, he is driving a gray digger on what is supposed to be another planet, or maybe the moon. I thought Erik's space-Lego was ugly and boring, it was all in shades of gray, and I had no interest in space, but maybe Nicholas would like to play with it now. If his grandma doesn't mind.

We are having a barbecue in the evening, all four of us help out. Nicholas is standing on a chair by the kitchen sink chopping up cucumber for the salad. The air is still warm and we are going to eat outside at the back, Mom and I carry out glasses and dishes, I cut up a store-bought baguette into thick, diagonal slices, wrap them in a tea towel in the breadbasket so they won't dry out, just like Mom used to do when I was little.

The food is nothing out of the ordinary but it's delicious, it tastes like it always used to. Nicholas eats his sausage and his cucumber salad, spreads a thick layer of margarine on his bread and munches happily. He is finished long before the rest of us, and tries to persuade someone to play hide-and-seek with him in the garden, but not even Dad, who usually says yes to everything Nicholas suggests, is prepared to interrupt dinner. Nicholas pulls a face.

"I remember one Christmas when we played hide-and-seek in the house," I say. "The two of you searched for Erik and me. You found me really quickly, then I helped you look for Erik. But we couldn't find him anywhere."

Neither Mom nor Dad says anything. Only when I hear my own words do I realize how they sound.

"Where was he hiding?" Nicholas wants to know.

"Behind a curtain in the living room," I say, a little more quietly. "We all thought it was strange, we should have seen his feet. In the end we had to ask him to come out. He was so proud of how well he'd hidden himself."

I give a faint smile, Mom shakes her head.

"I don't remember that," she says.

"Me neither." Dad reaches for the roasted vegetables. "These are very good—what seasoning did you use?"

"It's only thyme," I mumble.

"Well, it's very tasty."

Nicholas looks tired, he has started to sleep late since the start of the summer vacation, and today he was up earlier than usual. I recognize the signs. He soon becomes restless after he has finished eating, wriggles around on his chair even though he has been given his iPad and a little box of Zoo fruit candy.

"I'll take him in and put him to bed," I say after a while. The time is just after eight, the sky is still light. It is a lovely evening.

I brush Nicholas's teeth and fetch him a glass of water. The bed is made up with old, soft sheets, I remember them from when I was a child. Mom and Dad don't buy anything new unnecessarily. Not because they're mean, it's a kind of old-fashioned sensible thinking that is typical of their generation of Swedes. It is foolish to spend money on things that are not necessary. As long as the sheets have no holes in them, they will do perfectly well. However, if they were too shabby, or torn, they would be replaced immediately, because otherwise it would look as if you were poor. They have never really been poor, but they have never had a lot of money either. They saved anything that was left over when the necessities had been paid for.

I remember a few occasions from my childhood when a new purchase was in the cards, like when the old three-piece suite in the living room finally had to be changed, it was always a major event, preceded by a thorough investigation before a decision was made, whereupon that decision was presented as the most rational, in effect the only possible choice. As if every other suite were impractical, uneconomic, frivolous. It was a decision that had very little to do with form and almost everything to do with function, and even those aspects that were about form finally ended up as function. Did the color go with the rest of the décor? Was the fabric washable?

I often think somewhere deep down that that was where my attraction to the unnecessary was born. To things that lack function. To art.

We read the latest copy of Bamse the Bear, which I had brought along, a lengthy adventure about a wizard, then Nicholas falls asleep almost immediately. I sit for a while, just watching him. He is so like John. Their faces, powerful and open, and their bodies, strong and compact. Together they are an equally harmonious whole as John's boat, Nicholas is as clear a continuation of his father as the beautifully finished shelves and cupboards, as if John had crafted a son in his image.

I have sometimes wished that my only child were more like me, I have thought that it was a bad idea to reproduce with a man whose genes are so obviously dominant. I always push my concerns aside, feeling ashamed because they are both unpleasant and vain. Of course the most important thing is that my son is healthy, that he is happy, not that he looks like me. But occasionally, especially when he is about to fall asleep, I think he looks like Erik. When he loses control of his face and it becomes completely relaxed, there is something about the shape of his lips and the curve of his cheeks that means I see my brother's face pass over his, like a fleeting shadow.

I wish Mom and Dad could see it, see that there is a trace of Erik left behind, and that this is where it is.

There is something soft about the silence in the house on summer evenings. The smell of warm wood, the muted sounds outside, the gentle twilight slowly falling. Mom and Dad have come in, they are sitting on the sofa that dates back to the mid-90s. Behind them on the wall is one of my paintings, a large canvas that I gave them. It is one of the very few that don't represent mountains, but a sky. I did a series of skies as an experiment after I bought a book on Constable's studies of clouds, and became obsessed with them. I liked my cloud paintings when I did them, and I still liked them when they were exhibited, they were effective: an entire room that seemed to be full of windows looking out at the sky, with different cloud formations and ever-changing light.

But all by itself the painting looks nondescript. It shows fine weather, with fluffy, carefree clouds. I wanted to give Mom and Dad something beautiful and light, but it is a light that needs darkness, a sky that needs other skies in order to come into its own.

When I learned to talk about my mountains, at first I described the clouds as their contrast. I said the clouds were fleeting and transient, which was why so many artists had chosen to paint them. There was a temptation to try to capture the elusive. Even so many years after the breakthrough of the camera, when it was super-easy to paint from a photograph of a cloud, it still came across as more impressive to paint clouds than mountains.

The mountains seemed wooden, stiff in comparison. They stood where they stood. As if they lacked the soul and spirit often attributed to clouds.

That is a mistake, I said. The same mistake that is often made with people. We are drawn to those who are immediately charming, but many charming individuals are exactly like clouds. They will disperse over time. The more you get to know them, the clearer it becomes that they lack substance. People who are like ancient mountains, on the other hand... We should cling to them. And hope they want to cling to us too.

Sylvia was a mountain, I always thought. Solid and immovable. During my last year at Mejan we grew close, it was as if we both dropped our preconceived opinions of each other and realized that we were actually alike. After I finished my course we continued to meet up, sometimes for coffee or a glass of wine after visiting an exhibition together, but more often for dinner in her generous apartment on Sankt Paulsgatan, it was completely unrenovated and cluttered. Everything was ingrained, in a way that felt kind of cozy. Climbing potted plants had wound themselves around the curtain poles, presumably making it impossible to change the curtains, several piles of books had become surfaces on which to dump magazines, half-empty glasses and ashtrays. Sylvia still smoked indoors if she felt like it. The inside of the bathroom door was covered by a poster that was far from smooth because of the dampness, a still from a video where Sylvia stood dressed—or undressed—in thigh-high boots and a corset, with a beret on her head. STRIP TEASE it said in neon-pink capital letters at the top. It was her breakthrough piece, the image featured in several books on contemporary art, video art, and feminist art. It was a comment on male dominance in the industry, it was post-modernism, it was influenced by the medium of film and by Cindy Sherman, it ticked all the boxes at the time.

Syliva was still youthful in her sixties. It was only certain details that betrayed her age: the reading glasses she always wore on the top of her head when she was walking around at home, the fact that she sat down and spent some considerable time lacing up her shoes. She did it with some embarrassment, she never made an issue of her age, she would never have referred to herself as old, not even ironically.

She often cooked me something French. She had lived in Paris for many years when she was young, and she still loved French bistro food: croque madame and chèvre chaud, bouillabaisse, minute steak using good quality meat she bought in Södermalm. Bread with the meal, always a dessert. The wine was served in small round glasses, there was always a slightly washed-out cloth on the table, candles burned in wax-spattered brass candlesticks, it was all unexpectedly homey considering the fact that Sylvia often appeared quite hard.

Little by little I had realized that she wasn't hard at all, simply uninterested in anything she didn't think concerned her, which included most other people and most of the things that occupied them. I was one of the few who was let into her life in spite of everything, maybe because she understood that we were driven by the same aspiration, the same longing for something that was important for real.

Toward the end, when she was sick, she said she would really like to invite me to dinner but she wasn't strong enough to cook, so I invited her over to my place instead. I wasn't especially good at cooking, but somehow I got the idea that I ought to prepare something French for her, a boeuf bourguignon. It bubbled away for half a day, but I still thought the sauce was watery when it was ready, so I followed the recipe's suggestions on how to fix it. I must have done too much fixing, because it ended up glutinous, more like school canteen food than France.

Sylvia didn't have much of an appetite, but she said it was delicious. In spite of this, all I could think about during the evening was the fact that I had messed up the meal. And then, when she died, I couldn't stop thinking that the only thing I had done the last time we met was to brood over my awful stew. Among all the other reasons to hate death, it is particularly horrible when it puts its finger on your own imperfection.

After the funeral her brother contacted me to say that there was a folder of drawings that Sylvia had wanted me to have. They were from her student years, most probably from the Beaux Arts period, life drawings, a long series of beautifully drawn female bodies and a bundle of watercolor sketches, small landscapes reminiscent of the Impressionists' nature studies.

I began to talk to her sometimes, often when I was in the studio, even though she wasn't there.

"To think that you were an Impressionist," I said to her, gently teasing.

"That could have ended badly," she replied.

"You could have painted mountains day in and day out," I said.

"I guess there are worse things," she said and smiled, it was a warm smile that she bestowed only on certain people.

One of the watercolors was actually of a mountain, a French one, I framed the painting and hung it in the living room. The light and the vegetation were different, both lighter and brighter than in Sweden, but the mountain was just as gray as mine.

I have made painting relevant in today's society, according to a newspaper article after one of my first exhibitions. What a gift I have given to the world. It is a gift no one asked for, but everyone is happy to receive. The critics write what they need to write in order to remain relevant themselves, it doesn't matter to them if an artist's work is relevant or not, what matters is the ability to spin a story suggesting that it is. Then it becomes relevant, and they become relevant too. Everyone's a winner. Curators love everything that is relevant. Oh, the way they listen so sympathetically, their kindness. Their slightly too expensive interesting shoes and haircuts. Gallery owners also have an interest in money and know that paintings are easy to sell, even easier if you can also highlight their relevance to society. We are a community, all of us who are part of the system, a community with a conviction that painting is relevant as its foundation, a fleeting community that is over the day the interest on someone's part begins to fade, when times change, when another story becomes more powerful.

But I have a trump card. I have the grief over my brother who disappeared when I was a child, the grief I talked about in one of my first interviews, it wasn't planned, I just wasn't used to journalists and their questions, and I happened to answer with a little too much honesty. Then it became the keystone in my story.

That story is also a currency. All emotions and experiences can acquire a value if they are channeled into an expression: art ennobles elements that would otherwise appear base, trashy, tragic.

My parents' grief is worthless from that point of view, literally without value. It could have been exchanged for fifteen minutes in the spotlight if they had agreed to be interviewed by a tabloid newspaper or on the sofa on a morning TV show, weeping as they told a sympathetic reporter or host about their grief, about the emptiness Erik had left behind, about the terrible uncertainty, the desperation, about never getting closure. That is the opportunity on offer to ordinary people, to all those who have no other tools to legitimize their grief, to turn it into something that is taken seriously by the world.

My grief found an artistic expression, and therefore it was regarded as meaningful. It wasn't weepy and messy, simply quietly present, it was dignified and sophisticated, it lay beneath my paintings like a refined, muted sounding board, paintings that were good in their own right—technically, conceptually, in terms of form—but they were given additional weight if you knew my history, if you knew about the darkness that gave them an extra dimension, a dimension that made them into important works of art.

However, you had to understand the system. Art was meaningful only to someone who shared the belief that it meant something. Its emotions were relevant only to someone who had entered into the agreement that grief in art was different from grief in the tabloid press. It was a two-step system. Unlike money—money had only one step. Money was about money or no money.

Suddenly I had both. Not an excessive amount of money, but enough to live in a decent apartment in the center of Stockholm as a single mother, enough to do something unnecessary from time to time. More money than my parents had ever had.

They like the cloud painting. They prefer it to the mountains. Which isn't so hard to understand. Sometimes I worry that they will think I swapped my brother for art. Sometimes I think so myself—that he had to be sacrificed so that I could become what I have become. It is actually an illogical thought, but I think it anyway.

That he gave me a grief that saved me from becoming something I despise, a person who holds their finger in the air to gauge which way society's winds are blowing, opportunistic and politically correct. I don't need to be political, I have my wound.

"Did he fall asleep?" Mom asks when she sees me standing in the doorway.

"Yes, he was exhausted."

I join them on the sofa, the TV is on with the sound turned down low. It's a program with a group of Swedes—who I assume are famous—in the USA, in one of the southern states, they cook, play the guitar, talk things through with one another, it is in every way artificial and meaningless, but Mom and Dad seem to like it. After a while I go into the kitchen and make myself a cup of tea, then I sit down at the table and drink it while scrolling distractedly through my phone. Richard has sent another message: *Think about which painting we should use for the poster!*

The following morning Nicholas wakes just before eight, which is early for him, but he says he isn't sleepy and doesn't want to stay in bed. We go down to the kitchen, I turn on the coffee maker and make him a toasted sandwich, he eats it in front of an episode of *Sommarlov* on the iPad. After a while Mom and Dad appear, Dad takes Nicholas with him to fetch the newspaper.

“Can we go on the trampoline today?” Nicholas asks when they get back.

I have managed to suppress the invitation to use the trampoline, and have absolutely no desire to go over to the Ekmans.

“Maybe after lunch,” I say, hoping that he will have forgotten by then, even though I know he won’t. “Let’s go for a walk.”

He complains a little, but gives in. We head for the forest, it is only a few hundred yards away. The streets are narrower than I remember, the big crossroads down by the scout hut isn’t big at all and the asphalt looks new, dark, and smooth. The forest is different too, the trees are shorter and sparser, presumably they were thinned out many years ago.

“I’ll show you where our den used to be,” I say.

“Okay.”

My childhood exists in an abstract past as far as Nicholas is concerned, a distant era when there were landline telephones and animated movies hardly ever appeared on TV, an era that presumably seems as gray to him as the concept of my parents’ childhood seemed to me: all the stores were closed on Good Friday and only solemn music was played on the radio, but you could buy candy for next to nothing, a dizzying thought, and so it unfolds backward through time, a pearl necklace of templates, the joy and sorrow of generations reduced to a few simple, general facts, yet at the same time they were true and in their way more significant than what was regarded as really important, all the big stuff that was happening out in the world.

The idea of a den from the '80s seems old and boring to Nicholas, and it doesn't help when we discover that there is very little left of the place. I realize it wasn't actually much of a den, just a group of trees and a sort of roof between two piles of rocks. We could crawl in beneath the roof when the weather was wet, the branches Erik had arranged protected us pretty well from the wind and rain, and that was where we lay when it was night in our games, before we set off higher up into the forest to collect blueberries in the cone-shaped containers we made out of large maple leaves. In preparation for the winter, we said, because we were in the middle of a fantasy somewhere between the hunters and gatherers we had learned about in school, and the old agricultural Sweden that Grandma had told us about.

"Back in the day people really did have to gather food ready for the winter," I inform Nicholas, still without really knowing which "back in the day" I am talking about, but it doesn't really matter, it's true anyway. He nods.

"Like the squirrels," he says.

They learn a lot about nature at his preschool, or maybe he gets it from John.

"Exactly. But they often forget where they've hidden their nuts, and they spend hours searching for them."

"I know. They should keep everything in the same place."

"Although it's pretty clever, storing their nuts in different places," I say. "If they only had one store and another animal found it, they'd lose all their winter food in one go, and then they wouldn't have anything to eat."

He nods, thinks it over.

"They should have a better memory," he concludes.

"They should." I can't help laughing. "Shall we see if we can find some blueberries?"

He nods again and we head farther up into the forest, up toward the railway. The ground is sandier there and raspberries grow beside the path, tiny wild raspberries that are perfectly ripe. My stomach contracts when I taste the first one, it is like a concentrate of my childhood.

"Aren't they delicious?" I say. "I think wild raspberries are much nicer than the ones you get in the garden. They have more flavor, somehow."

"Yummy," Nicholas agrees. He doesn't stop eating until we have picked all the ripe ones we can reach, and in desperation he even eats a couple that are unripe.

We continue along the path, up to the railway crossing. All the wild strawberries that used to grow there are gone, maybe they cleared them away when the railway was renovated—the metal barriers look brand-new, and the concrete slabs between the tracks are pale and clean.

"This is the way our train came," I say. "Do you remember me telling you? When I was little I wasn't allowed to cross here. I can understand why, it can be really dangerous if a train comes along. Then I had a friend who lived on the other side, so I had to learn what to do. You have to look and listen really carefully."

Nicholas seems to be taking what I say very seriously.

"So how old were you then?" I think for a moment then say "Nine, maybe" to make it clear that such a thing lies far in the future for him. In fact I was no more than seven. If that.

He tucks his hand in mine. "Can we go across?"

"Absolutely. But we have to look and listen really carefully."

We go through the barriers and up to the track, the gravel crunches beneath my feet just as it always did, we look to the right and the left twice, we keep very quiet and listen hard. There is no sound from the tracks.

"Okay, we can go across," I whisper without really knowing why, everything seems somehow ceremonial. Nicholas scampers over and through the barriers on the other side, he turns around and grins at me as if we have just done something tremendously exciting.

"My friend lived just up the hill," I say, pointing along the road.

"Shall we go and see if she's home?" Nicholas asks.

"It was a he. Marcus. But he won't be home. He doesn't live here anymore."

Nicholas continues up the hill anyway, as if he senses that I don't want him to, but that I have no good reason to stop him. So I follow him. Along the path, then there's the house on the left, still pink, but smaller than

I remember. The fruit trees have grown, they look as if they've stood there forever. The lawn is still neatly cut, and it is still cluttered with plastic toys.

"A pink house—how pretty!" Nicholas says.

"Yes, it's quite unusual."

We have been standing there for less than a minute. Nicholas has commented on a scooter by the gate, when suddenly we hear a sound and the patio door opens. A woman steps out, smiling broadly. I recognize Kicki right away. She is older, but she still has the same aura, I can see it even from this distance.

"Hanna!" she calls out, sounding delighted. "It is you, isn't it?"

"It is."

She slides her feet into a pair of garden clogs by the door and hurries across the patio and the lawn. She hugs me tightly, she smells exactly the same as she used to, the faint scent of a warm, spicy perfume, I think it's Montana, I immediately recall the frosted glass bottle on the bathroom shelf.

"And who's this?" she asks, looking at Nicholas. He is suddenly shy, but pleased.

"This is Nicholas."

"My name is Kicki. I knew your mom when she was a little girl. When she was about the same age as you, in fact."

He nods, his expression serious as he takes in this information.

"So how are you?" Kicki goes on. "You could come in for something to eat and drink, but we're just about to go out. Have you spoken to Marcus?"

She asks the question as if she thinks we're in touch, as if we speak from time to time, keep our relationship going, make plans to meet. I don't have the heart to tell her we haven't been in touch for twenty years.

"No. It's been a while, to be honest."

"They're here," she says, "they're at the zoo with the kids, but they'll be back this afternoon. I'll send him down to your place after dinner. You have to meet up while you're both here."

She looks happy. She has aged, but in an enviable way that suggests she has hardly noticed, and doesn't intend to waste energy worrying about it. Whenever I was in their house, during all those years, she was so kind to me. Even with two small children, she always found time to talk to me. Somehow she always pitched it at the right level, unlike almost everyone else, both children and adults, she was better at it than the adults who were trained in that field although she was a hairdresser—or maybe that was exactly why. No prying questions about Erik, she never made me feel under pressure to provide answers or reactions or explanations, she just gave me warmth and understanding, a wordless assurance that she too knew what life could bring. Why don't we know each other any longer? She's the kind of person I ought to send a Christmas card to at least. Then again, I never send Christmas cards. I should start, for her sake.

"Absolutely," I say, "That would be great."

She gives me another hug. "I have to dash—how long are you staying?"

"A few more days, I guess."

"Come back and have coffee!" she says, pretending to sound stern. "Promise!"

I nod, she smiles and hurries back indoors.

"She was nice," Nicholas says.

"She was."

I can't get what she said about Marcus out of my mind. *They're here.* That means he's here with his family, maybe a large family by now, a whole gang of children, at least three, middle-class families always have three children. It doesn't match the image I had when I googled him, which I have done at regular intervals. He is no longer on the university's home page, and there is nothing to indicate that he completed his doctorate. I haven't been able to work out what job he does, and there are no social media accounts in his name. All that exists are his name and date of birth on sites with personal information, and according to them he lives in an apartment in central Malmö. Unmarried, no one else registered at that address, no car, no dog, no involvement in any companies. But maybe there's some practical or legal reason—an apartment in Malmö that he doesn't want to sell, so he keeps it as his registered address even though he actually lives in a large house on the outskirts of Lund with his family, I make a quick calculation and realize that he could have a child aged about twenty, maybe he or she lives in the apartment, but then again a twenty-year-old probably wouldn't want to go to the zoo, so there must be younger children too, perhaps he has children with two different women, small children with a younger woman, he has brought them to his mom's on vacation. Almost half our lives have passed since we last saw each other. In many ways I am a different person now. It is uncomfortable to think that maybe he is too.

"Mom?" Nicholas says in a challenging tone.

"Sorry?" I didn't hear what he said.

"Can I go and play on the trampoline now?"

Once I've started thinking about him, I can't stop. Nicholas and I go home and I make a quick lunch, macaroni with meatballs for him and a tuna sandwich for me, we sit in the kitchen even though the weather is lovely and we ought to sit out, I can't face carrying everything outside. Mom and Dad are busy in the vegetable patch, they come in after a while and start warming up some leftover pie. I tell them I met Kicki. They say they sometimes bump into her, she and Bengt are still together, who would have thought it. I can't work out if their tone is one of sympathy or reluctant admiration.

After lunch Nicholas and I go over to the Ekmans and ring the bell. They answer the door together, curious, pleased to see us. How Nicholas has grown! Would he like to try out the trampoline? It's a shame their grandchildren aren't here at the moment, they're coming next week, but maybe we will have left by then? We are so lucky with the weather. Have we been swimming yet? Nicholas gets upset because we haven't gotten around to it, he makes me promise we can go tomorrow. Apparently the water in Lilla Älgsjön is lovely and warm right now, we ought to make the most of it. I promise that we will make the most of it. *Has Marcus been swimming?* I wonder. Marcus and the children. Marcus and the family. Marcus and his partner. Or wife. What does she look like? What do they talk about? What do they laugh at? What do they have in common?

Nicholas bounces like crazy, I shout to him several times telling him to take it easy, but he ignores me. In the end I yell that he could break a leg or an arm, it will really hurt and he'll have to wear a cast and he won't be able to swim all summer. He calms down a little, but soon he is calling to me to check this out as he does an extra high leap and spins around in the air, he wants me to film him, and clap, so I do. I'm not even sure how we know the Ekmans. Maybe Mom knows fru Ekman from the sewing circle, I think they both used to be members. Mom and Dad have dinner with the Ekmans from time to time, but they started socializing after I left home, so to me their friendship feels new.

It might be a good thing if Nicholas tires himself out on the trampoline, maybe he will go to sleep early this evening. Before Marcus comes by. If he comes by. So I can talk to Marcus alone. Unless he brings the family. I hope to God he doesn't bring the family. What shall I wear? I haven't brought many clothes with me. But I did pack a dress, I'll wear that.

Once again Nicholas wants me to "Check this out!" as he does his hundredth bounce and spins in the air, I look, I applaud distractedly, take out my phone to see how late it is. Will I have time to wash my hair? I will have time to wash it, but will it have time to dry? What are we eating tonight? Probably barbecue again. Fru Ekman comes out with a bottle of Fanta and two glasses just as I am about to suggest we say our goodbyes and head home, Nicholas scrambles down from the trampoline and quickly drinks one glass, belches, laughs, apologizes, and scrambles back up again. Fru Ekman laughs too, nodding at him. It's amazing how long it can keep them occupied. Indeed it is. I sit down in the shade next to some currant bushes, the squeaking of the trampoline is starting to get on my nerves. I tell Nicholas we will be going home soon, he howls in protest, it's too early, we never do anything fun, which is a lie, we are going swimming tomorrow. Fru Ekman has heard us and comes out again, says we are welcome to come back whenever we like, it's lovely to have us here.

I thank her for the use of the trampoline and for the soda, Nicholas thanks her too, says it was so cool, then we head home. The asphalt is warm, in some places the tar has melted, become shiny and glutinous. Nicholas is fascinated, he shouts that the ground is bleeding, he grabs a stick and starts poking at a black patch, I tell him not to get it on his clothes, it will never come out I say, I can hear Mom's words in my voice and then I regret it, I suddenly remember how riveting melted asphalt used to be, so I too find a stick and we poke at it together. The smell of warm asphalt belongs to a particular category of childhood smells—the garage at home, the gas station, the jetty, lighter fluid and the lawnmower, the male, chemical smells, all enjoyable in their own special way.

Nicholas lies down on the sofa with his iPad when we get home, he is tired after all that bouncing. We are having barbecued salmon with potato salad, Mom tells me when I ask, Nicholas shouts that he hates fish, it is as if the initial politeness has drained away and he has started to behave more like he does at home. I point out that his comment wasn't very nice and he certainly does not hate fish, but by then Mom has already said that there are sausages left over and before I have time to say that he had sausages yesterday, he shouts that he will have them instead of fish. I wonder what Marcus and his family are having. They're probably barbecuing too. Will Bengt be in charge? No doubt he has bought a big, expensive barbecue, maybe one that runs on gas. Will he be cooking burgers for everyone? And joking that he is still the Burger King?

I go upstairs to change. I feel a little foolish, but if Marcus does drop by, I want him to think I look nice. I have always wanted him to think I look nice. I am more attractive now than I used to be, at least for my age, I was a reasonably attractive teenager but now I am more attractive than many women in their forties. Not that it matters, says my brain, a boring part of my brain, of course it matters says another, I apply blush to my cheeks, touch up my mascara, put on my gold hoop earrings. I haven't washed my hair but it looks good, good enough anyway.

The salmon is delicious, even Nicholas eats a little, I remain at the table after dinner while he builds an obstacle course from some planks of wood and buckets on the grass, I pour myself a glass of wine and sip it slowly. It is another lovely evening. How many lovely summer evenings do we get in life? I remember when they used to seem endless, during the summer vacations when I was a teenager, one evening after another, it felt as if it would always be like that.

I put Nicholas to bed, he wants a story before he goes to sleep, so I tell him about a squirrel who lives by the den in the forest, he has forgotten where he has hidden his nuts for the winter, Nicholas laughs, the story seems to have livened him up, but he soon falls asleep anyway. He isn't used to being outside all day long, the fresh air has tired him out.

I have told Mom and Dad that Marcus is going to stop by, and asked them to keep an eye on Nicholas. When it is almost nine o'clock I go and sit on the wall at the front of the house, scrolling aimlessly on my phone, the evening papers, social media, it is quarter past nine and suddenly he is standing there.

He is bigger than I remember. Heavier. Something has happened to his face, his features used to be so sharply delineated, I was fascinated because it almost looked as if it had been drawn, clear lines along his jaw and cheekbones. Those lines have softened now, kind of dissolved. It is as if his gaze has also softened, as if something within him has settled. Or given up.

"Hanna," he says. His smile is a little shy.

"Hi," I say, I stand up and he gives me a hug. It is strange to feel his body next to mine, familiar and unfamiliar at the same time.

"How are you?" he says, because that's what people say.

"Fine," I say, because that is also what people say.

We both smile, conscious of the predictability of the situation, he sits down beside me and I search my brain for something better to say, but as usual he gets there first.

"Mom said...," he begins, breaks off, "Mom said you have a son."

"Nicholas. Yes."

"Fantastic. Any more?"

"Children? No, only him. His dad and I aren't together anymore."

The last sentence slips out and I am embarrassed: it is a piece of information I should have kept back for the time being if I didn't want to sound desperate, and I am not desperate, just nervous. He doesn't give any indication that I have said something weird. Maybe he is nervous too.

"How about you?"

"No," he says. "No kids. I'm . . . What do people say these days? Single? I live alone."

"Right," I say, I can hear the surprise in my voice. "How come?"

"It hasn't gone too well when I've tried living with someone. And I've tried several times. I even got married. And divorced."

"I haven't gotten any further than a separation."

He gives me a fleeting smile. "In that case I'm in the lead," he says.

He is wearing a shirt that is too big, I find it quite touching. As if he thinks the shirt will hide the fact that he has put on weight, or because he wants to cover up, maybe he's not used to his body and thinks he needs bigger clothes than is actually the case. He used to dress so well, mainly in black, it's strange to see him like this. Slightly lost in a big pale shirt. Around his neck I see the glint of a small cross on a silver chain.

"I thought . . ." I begin. "I mean, Kicki said you were at the zoo with the kids, so I thought . . . you had kids."

"They're Victor's and Amanda's. They've got two each."

"What?"

He laughs. "They're not so little anymore."

"I can't believe they've got kids—the last time I saw them they were children themselves."

"They're both in their thirties."

I shake my head. "That's insane," I murmur.

He clears his throat. "I see you're doing well. You've got a big exhibition coming up soon, haven't you?"

"I have, at Liljevalchs. It opens in September."

"It would be cool to see it," he says.

I nod. "You must get in touch if you come to Stockholm."

It all sounds so hollow. Like something you just say, something that is never going to happen.

"So how about you—are you still at the university?" I ask.

"No, that didn't go too well either."

"What happened?"

"It just... I never finished my thesis. The problem is... well, I drank a little too much for too many years. It started when I was working on my thesis."

He shrugs, he seems embarrassed but determined not to keep it a secret.

"It turns out that alcoholism is hereditary."

"What? Who's an alcoholic? Kicki never drank much, did she?"

"Dad, of course. I know you got the idea that he's some kind of successful academic, but that was never true. He did his job badly for years, but they kept him on until he was eligible for his pension just to be kind. The students liked him. But he's hopeless. And then it turned out that I'm hopeless too."

He gives me a wan smile.

"I work at a high school. It's not too bad, it's in town so it's pretty calm. Hardworking students. I teach mainly religion, plus a little history and Swedish. It's okay. And Malmö is okay."

"Better than here?" I say.

"I don't know, is Stockholm better than here?"

"I don't know."

"What do any of us fucking know?" he says. "We think we can be whatever we want, whoever we want, and then we discover that we definitely can't. Do you remember? When it felt as if life lay before us like a buffet, and all we had to do was make a choice, help ourselves? Move here or there, do this or that. Do you remember how much I talked about what I was going to do? And then I found there wasn't much choice after all. Almost as if everything was preordained."

There is a strand of bitterness in his voice that wasn't there before.

"It was because you always said you were going to leave that I started to believe I could do it too," I say. "But I hated it when you talked about it. I had to make a huge effort not to protest every time you said you were going to leave, and talked about everything you were going to do."

He looks at me, he is clearly surprised. How strange, I think, that we were such a big part of each other's lives, and yet we never discussed it, never acknowledged with a single word that we were important to each other. Everything simply existed, simultaneously unspoken and obvious.

"Do you realize how hard I had to try not to be jealous of like, everyone?" I say. "Nearly all the girls were in love with you at some point during high school."

He smiles, looks embarrassed.

"I made an effort for you too," he says. "I took you to Bengt's restaurant."

"Once! Once in all those years!"

He laughs. "I fought for your sake." His tone is more serious now.

He did. I still remember it clearly, how shocked I was, I didn't know he could fight, and I'd never seen violence in real life before. I remember the dull, kind of meaty sound of his fist connecting with Albin's face, the blood flowing. The whole thing was horrible, revolting, yet strangely satisfying.

"True. Nobody's done that for me since then."

"I haven't had a fight since then either."

"Good," I say, because of course it's stupid to fight, but maybe mostly because I like knowing that I'm the only one he's fought for.

"So . . ." he says, standing up and kicking at the gravel by the roadside. "Shall we do something? I don't suppose you'd like to come home with me? Meet everyone?"

I would, but not now. Not yet. I want him to myself for a while longer.

"I haven't been anywhere since we got here," I say. "Can we go somewhere else? How about a bike ride?"

"Fine."

He follows me to the garage and helps me open the door, which is quite stiff. I switch on the fluorescent light, it flickers and frightens a moth, which flutters away into a corner. The bikes are in a tangled heap. Marcus takes Dad's, an old green Monark. Erik's bike is still there, pale blue with a metallic finish and racing handlebars. The police brought it back when the forensic examination was finished. Dad put it in the garage, and I guess it's been here ever since. They probably thought a spare bike might be useful. Or maybe they thought Nicholas would be able to use it when we come to stay in the future. Or else they didn't think at all, they couldn't cope with thinking about everything. My tires need pumping up, so I take Mom's bike instead, it's sturdy, lilac, just a few years old. She's the only one who still cycles on a regular basis.

Marcus sets off ahead of me, moving fast. We head for Hyttan, then down past the old market garden, the road sweeps around the village past fields and pastureland with a farm in the middle, high on a hill, a relic of the past. I have never cycled so late before but the sky is still light, the road follows the rolling landscape, up and down, the birch trees line the route, ghostly white. Once we pass the rectory it is downhill all the way to Bråviken. At the crossroads by the campsite he stops at last and gets off his bike.

"Where are we going?" I ask.

"I don't know. But I thought... I mean I don't know, but have you been there since it happened? To the mountain?"

The road we are on continues to Mount Verity, it isn't far, and it won't be dark for a while yet.

"I was there with Mom once, but it's a long time ago."

"Shall we?"

I can't decide if this is a good or a bad idea. Maybe neither. If I'm ever going to go there again, this might be a good opportunity.

"Okay. Let's do it. Let's go to Mount Verity."

Marcus nods, gets back on his bike and starts pedaling. It's uphill for a short distance, a sharp bend, then downhill again, we pass the turnoff for the marble works, everything feels so easy. The summer evening is warm and pale, the breeze ruffles my hair, I turn my face up to it, my bicycle slicing through the mild air.

Soon we are passing the zoo and the big parking lot, which is deserted at this time. Marcus brakes.

"So how did you get along with learning to drive?" he says.

"Not too well."

"You really ought to do it, you know."

I suddenly remember how things ended that time he took me out to teach me. How he drove up to the TV mast afterward, how cold his hands were on my breasts when he stood behind me in the forest and slipped them beneath my top. I look at him and I can see that he is thinking the same thing, he gives me a wry smile and sets off again.

The forest is dark all around us, there are no lights after the zoo. Only forest all the way down to the water on one side of the road, and all the way up to Södermanland on the other. The taillight of Marcus's bicycle is winking at me like a red eye.

He stops on a bend.

"It's here, isn't it?" he says.

The bend is extra wide and has a sign with M on it—meeting place. A path leads into the forest.

"I don't know."

I haven't been to the mountain since Mom and I went there, it's a long time ago.

"Shouldn't there be a sign or something if it is here?" I say.

"What kind of sign?"

"To say it's a historic site or a tourist attraction or something."

"I think you need genuine history for one of those," Marcus says. "All the stories about Mount Verity are only rumors, even if they are old."

He gets off his bike and pushes it a few yards into the forest, then props it up against a tree. "Coming?"

I get off my bike, prop it up next to his. Then I follow him in among the tree trunks. It is dark, but my eyes soon get used to it and the path is well-trodden, the ground seems to give beneath my feet. The forest, still equally familiar and incomprehensible. When I was little I thought that I was a part of it, that we knew each other. That nature was a language I understood, and could speak. Then Erik disappeared and it became something else. Nature and I no longer knew each other, that's how it feels. It was stupid to believe we ever did.

Soon the path begins to climb, the ground is firmer, we are on the mountain now. I keep my eyes fixed on Marcus's back, he stops and bends a spindly pine sapling to one side for me. It gets lighter the higher up we go, the trees are sparser. He holds out his hand and helps me up the last section.

Then we are standing side by side at the top of Mount Verity. Before us lie the dark waters of Bråviken and then the Vikbolandet peninsula, to the right we can just make out the lights of Norrköping.

A short distance away lies the opening of the cave, like a dark eye in the mountain. Marcus goes over to it and looks down, comes back and sits down. I sit beside him. The surface of the smooth rock is still warm, it has been gathering the heat of the sun all day, but despite this I am suddenly frozen, I think I can feel the cave staring at my back.

"I've dreamed about this place so many times," I say. "That I'm here, searching for him. That he's still down there inside the mountain, and can't come home with me."

I feel the tears scalding my eyes.

"It's just a dream," Marcus says.

"But it must mean something."

"In that case I think it's more about you than Erik."

"What do you mean?"

"Maybe it's about your feelings of guilt?" he ventures.

"Right."

I suddenly feel stupid. Of course he's right. He's still always right. Maybe it is all about me, and nothing to do with Erik any longer. That's also a reason to feel guilty. There is always a reason to feel guilty.

"Why did you never get in touch?" I ask.

I don't mean to sound accusatory, but I guess I do. Now he's here, sitting next to me, it seems bizarre that he hasn't done it for so many years.

He looks down.

"You must realize," he says quietly.

And in that moment I do: because he's ashamed. Because he is where I was the last time we met, because he is the one who feels like a failure in comparison to me right now. It is such an alien thought that it has never even occurred to me before. The idea that Marcus could think that I am somehow in a superior position, that he might even be afraid of disappointing me.

"If Mom hadn't nagged me I wouldn't have come to see you today either," he adds.

"So we would have spent the rest of our lives without any contact at all?" I realize my tone is still a little accusatory. "Even though we are sometimes only a few hundred yards apart?"

"Probably, yes."

"Why?" I say.

He shrugs. "So why haven't you been in touch?"

Yes, why haven't I? Because I thought he was living a life where there was no room for me. Because I thought it would be difficult for him if I got in touch, that it would complicate his life in a way that would be better avoided. And because I thought he was busy with something better, something more important.

He gives a wan smile when I tell him this.

"I haven't done anything important for a long time."

"I don't believe that," I say, because you have to protest when someone says something like that, even though it's possible that he might be right to some extent. "I mean, surely it depends what you think is important," I go on, but it sounds anything but sincere. I clear my throat. "I hope you get to do something important soon."

"Me too."

I lean back and lie down. I can feel the warmth on my back and my arms through my clothes. I try to draw it into my body. The sky is pale blue, still too light for any stars to show. Do you ever see stars in the summer? How can I possibly not remember? How can I have lived this long and not know something like that?

"Can you hear anything?" I say.

He looks at me.

"Voices," I go on. "Apparently you're supposed to be able to hear women's voices here at night."

"Oh, that. I've never believed that."

"People claim to have heard them."

"People claim all kinds of things. If you know you can hear them, then you're going to believe you can hear them."

I sit up again. "Shouldn't you be the one who believes in that kind of thing? You with your open mind to all that mysterious stuff?"

He smiles. "I'm selective about what I believe these days."

"And of all the things you could believe in, you chose God." I nod to the cross around his neck.

Reflexively his hand reaches up to touch it.

"I suppose I thought it was the least bad alternative," he says.

The forest around us has darkened, the trees stand like black silhouettes against the sky.

"I just don't understand how believing in God helps," I say. "When things still just happen without our being able to control them. It seems a bit desperate to believe there's some kind of meaning in it all. Or a bit sad. Delusional."

"What's wrong with being delusional?"

"I think you have to live a true life," I say. "Pure. Or honest, at least."

"I think most people who believe in a god feel that way too."

I run my hand over the lichen, it is cinder lichen, the most common. And yet you are hardly aware that it exists, it is so like the rock it grows on that you often don't notice it. But I have painted it many times. I know that its structure is different from the rock's, it captures the light in a different way, absorbs it with its finely granulated, rough surface.

“I didn’t get confirmed,” I tell him. “Of course I didn’t. The very thought of it was kind of disgusting, partly because it was connected with the way Erik disappeared, and partly because it seemed to me that there’s something sick about a god who makes such a song and dance about letting his son rise from the dead, then takes my brother on the same night. Why would I want to believe in him? And I also think it’s too simple—having a formula for your whole life, always having an explanation for everything you don’t understand. And the explanation is always that there is some god or other who has a purpose in whatever happens. It seems kind of self-righteous to me.”

For once it’s nice to talk.

“I read an article about Neanderthals a while ago,” I continue. “For a long time it was assumed that they didn’t have a culture in the sense that *Homo sapiens* did. No doubt people were of the opinion that something like art would be too sophisticated for them. But a few years ago they realized that the paintings in a cave in Spain were much older than they’d thought—sixty-five thousand years old. At that time *Homo sapiens* hadn’t even arrived in Europe. So it was the Neanderthals who did those paintings. And they really made an effort, some of them are so deep within a cave system that there is no daylight at all. That means they must have taken fire with them in order to be able to paint.”

“What are the paintings of?”

"Most are some sort of abstract pattern made with dots. And there are handprints. But the strangest is a motif that doesn't exist in any later cave paintings—it looks as if they painted a ladder."

"A ladder?"

"Yes. Well, I mean there were no ladders in those days, so it was probably supposed to represent something else, but it really does look like a ladder. Don't you think there's a wonderful symbolism there? To belong to a human species that is dying out, and to paint a ladder? It's like the image of a completely impossible longing to climb higher in evolution. Up toward the light. Up out of the cave."

"In the Bible the ladder connects humankind with God," Marcus informs me.

I shake my head, he smiles.

"Okay, how about this then. In Celtic Christianity they talk about something called thin places. These are places where the boundary between God and man, or the spiritual and the earthly, however you want to put it, is unusually thin, enabling you to catch a glimpse of something divine—or whatever you wish to call it. Something dizzying, something sublime. Something that is greater than the here and now. It is often mountains that are spoken of as thin places. Mountains and caves."

"When I paint I always think it's like entering a cave," I say. "I'm really going into myself, but following a path inward, backward. Into something dark. If you understand what I mean."

He nods.

"Did you know that mountains also have a life cycle? Various geological processes are constantly taking place, which means that the types of mountains change. They metamorphose into one another, become part of one another. They cease to exist in one form, and begin to exist in a different form. Seen over an expanse of time that we are incapable of perceiving, you can actually say that the mountain lives."

I am trying to quote from memory the text that Sylvia wrote for my first exhibition, I'm not sure it's correct, but on the other hand I'm not completely sure that it was correct to start with. But it sounds good. It sounds true.

"I didn't know that."

"So it means that in a way, life is ultimately a question of time perspective. Time can both destroy and create life."

"Although a mountain isn't alive," he says, "because it isn't an organism. It is literally dead material."

"You of all people shouldn't object to the idea that something that was believed to be dead could live," I say.

He laughs. A pale moon is rising above Vikbolandet, almost full, it looks virtually transparent.

"What if they killed Erik too," I say. "What if it was like they said, they made him climb down into the cave and the mountain . . . took him. Because there's something down there, something old that has remained. Or maybe it was his friends. Some kind of mass psychosis, they egged one another on and he somehow died, it might not have been their intention. And then they panicked and worked together to hide the body. They might have dragged it down to Bråviken and dumped it in the water. They agreed to lie, to say that no one remembered anything. Or perhaps they really didn't remember. Because they were in shock."

"I think he would have been found if that were the case," Marcus says quietly. "Or the police would at least have found some traces in the forest. And traces on those who were with him, on their clothes. Blood or fragments of skin or strands of hair, something like that."

"Of all the people who are reported missing every year, and there are lots of them, several thousand, around thirty are never found," I inform him. "About half of them are asylum seekers who choose to disappear. And of the rest, most are individuals with serious problems, loners, addicts, the mentally ill. People with no family or friends. It might be a designated social worker or their guardian who discovers that they are gone, long after they actually disappeared. There is hardly anyone like Erik. What happened to him happens to hardly anyone. I can't get my head around the fact that he disappeared and I'm still here. It doesn't make any sense. It's like a vacuum."

He places his hand on mine, it is warm. He is always warm. Even back in high school I was always cold and he was warm, he was the one who had to warm me up when I was shivering.

"The afternoon before he disappeared we lay on the sofa in the living room each reading a Donald Duck comic book. Erik was reading one of my favorite adventures, a kind of Sherlock Holmes paraphrase where Mickey Mouse and Goofy are in London. The best thing about it was that you could decide how the story developed and ended. 'If you want Mickey to open the door, go to page fifty-two, if you want him to go through the tunnel instead, go to page sixty-five.' You know?"

He nods.

"I've thought about that so many times," I go on. "That that's how life works. Every little detail in our everyday lives affects other details, every small action is a choice that can have terrible consequences. It's dreadful when you start to think about it. What if Erik hadn't gone out with his friends that evening? What if they hadn't gone to the church? What if they hadn't cycled to the mountain? Then I would still have a brother. I've gone over that afternoon in my head so many times. What if it had snowed, like Mom thought it was going to? Then maybe they would have stayed indoors."

The movie in my mind starts up as soon as I say those words. The bobbled fabric of the sofa in the living room, its brown and orange pattern, Mom's voice from the room next door. The special light when it is overcast in the spring, when the sky is basically light, the dark clouds lit from behind, like a stage backdrop. I have tried to paint it, but it is difficult. Somehow it is more a feeling than a fact, the knowledge that the lighter time of year is on its way back, it is in my head but it is hard to capture on canvas. I picture Erik getting to his feet, going upstairs. The sound of his footsteps on the staircase is so familiar that I hardly hear it. In my room the tape is still running even though the Top 20 countdown must have finished. Erik walking around, Erik glancing into my room and seeing, or hearing, that the tape machine is still recording.

Why has this never occurred to me before? He was alone upstairs for a while with my cassette player. He could have gone into my room, switched off both the recording and the radio, then pressed Record and left a message for me. Just like he did on my name day, when he whispered my name and frightened me at first, before cheerfully shouting his congratulations.

I realize the idea is a long shot, but it is new, and every new idea is a new possibility. If he wasn't swallowed up by the mountain, if his friends didn't somehow manage to make him disappear without a trace, then there is a chance that he stood in my room and knew what was going to happen after midnight mass, because he himself had planned it.

Suicide is the most common cause of death among young men, the words echo inside my head, I have read it many times but always pushed the thought away because it is so grotesque, now I follow it through for the first time. Mom and Dad must have thought it too without mentioning it to me, because I was a child, maybe they didn't even articulate it to each other, from a sense of shame that they didn't want me to have to carry: the shame of having a brother who took his own life because he was the school's gay boy. And then there would have been their own shame at not having realized, not being able to help him. Layer upon layer of shame, like the rings on a tree trunk.

If he was the one who wanted to go to the mountain, then he could also have decided to give me, if not an explanation, then something to hold on to. Something that would make everything less incomprehensible.

That afternoon, when he had gone out, I went up to my room. I listened to the recording, but only until Kaj Kindvall said thank you and goodbye, and the Top 20 was over. Then I turned the tape over and rewound it, played a few tracks, and then I never listened to it again. I put it in a box in my closet and tried to forget that it existed, because it felt tainted, every single track bore witness to the appalling fact that suddenly my brother no longer existed. Presumably it is still there in the box in the closet, and there is a section of it that I have never listened to.

Marcus is talking about something, but I can't hear what he is saying, all I can think of is that I have to go home and I have to find the tape.

I cycle back in silence, with grim determination, and now I am the one in front. I sense Marcus behind me like a shadow while my brain works at full tilt, I can see everything so clearly, and I realize that if I find the tape and if there actually is a final message from Erik it will be over thirty years old and his voice will be that of a teenager, a boy speaking from the past.

We put the bikes back in the garage, I am stressed and clumsy and I know Marcus notices, but he doesn't ask any questions. Before we part he gives me a hug and I get the same feeling I have always had every time he has hugged me: I want to disappear into him, be enveloped by him, be absorbed by his calmness.

"Don't forget you're coming over for coffee," he says, "or Mom will never forgive you. Call me tomorrow."

It's a long time since anyone asked me to call them tomorrow, at least someone who doesn't specifically want something from me. Maybe he does, but maybe I want him to want something from me.

I slide my key into the lock as quietly as I can, take off my shoes and creep up the stairs. I still know exactly where they creak, which part of which stair I need to avoid so that I don't wake anyone. Nicholas is fast asleep in my bed, his breathing is calm and regular, I cautiously open the closet door, take out the box of cassette tapes without making a sound, use the light on my phone to see what's there.

The list of contents on each tape is messy, in my childish, rounded handwriting. I quickly rummage through them, and when I find the right tape I recognize it immediately: the case is transparent, which felt new and modern back then. BASF it says in capital letters, "Top 20 Easter Saturday 1989" on the label in turquoise felt-tip pen.

My old headphones are still lying beside the stereo. Both the synthetic leather and the foam rubber are dry and crumbly, but they still seem to work. When I switch on the stereo and plug them in, I hear a promising crackle.

I am perfectly well aware of how stupid it is to hope, and yet I still do it, it is a feverish, intoxicating hope that makes my hands shake as I insert the cassette into the tape deck and close the lid with a resistance that is so familiar, a soft click I have heard a thousand times. The tape hasn't been rewound, so when I press Play it begins in the middle of Debbie Gibson's "Lost in Your Eyes." It's a song I had almost forgotten about, but I remember it instantly, a ballad with a piano accompaniment and a voice that couldn't belong anywhere other than the late '80s. It breaks off abruptly before the track is over, and there is a crackling noise in my headphones for a few seconds before another song begins equally suddenly, "This Time I Know It's for Real" by Donna Summer, a cheerful, upbeat Stock Aitken Waterman intro, just the way it sounded on Easter Saturday afternoon in 1989.

It is such a long time ago. People who are adults now weren't even born then. Sometimes I wonder if it is still Erik I am mourning, or if I am mourning the fact that time passes. The fact that every little moment, everything that combines to make up the majority of our existence, simply disappears, dissolves, is forgotten.

With hindsight perhaps it seems as if life had a narrative. As if it had contours, something that held it together. I remember the first time I saw the Impressionists' paintings, I thought: "How can this be a picture? It's just a collection of patches." It's the same with life. How can this be a life, it's just a collection of events, a collection of memories, a collection of moments. How can this form a whole?

It is like looking up at the sky and seeing a cluster of stars, far far away, they are barely visible when you look straight at them, but if you allow your gaze to rest just beside them, they appear clearly in your peripheral vision, that is where they acquire a meaning: the huckleberries on the way to school, cracking the first ice that has formed overnight on a puddle, the special sound when it breaks, a sound that is unlike anything else, the dense grayness of a November morning, a sandwich for breakfast, the checkered front of the school piano on the morning of St. Lucia's day, Beatrix Potter's dancing animals on the day before Christmas Eve, the spent New Year rockets like treasure that has fallen from the sky, the flowers by the roadside and the field of wood anemones in the ravine down by the stream, the hedgehog rustling around under the patio one spring, we fed it liver pâté until it almost became tame, the fishing rods made out of branches, their cut surfaces smelling green and pure, of life and chlorophyll, we never caught any fish but it didn't matter, the cherry tree on the wasteland, the stick insect that disappeared in the garden, we mourned it together, sharing a pack of GB ice cream and eating it with a spoon straight out of the box in front of the TV, lying head-to-toe at opposite ends of the sofa, each reading an old Donald Duck comic book.

The smallest is the greatest. Once I had a brother, I think. Once we had the greatest.

I listen to the Top 20 all the way through and I hear Kaj Kindvall say thank you and goodbye, he is followed by the news, the news anchor's voice sounds old-fashioned, stern and dispassionate, then there is a concert, some kind of Christian pop, I wait for the interruption that is bound to come, the crackling and rushing sound before Erik's voice takes over, but suddenly the tape stops halfway through a chorus and there is silence.

There is nothing else on it except for the station P3's Easter Saturday afternoon offering. Of course there isn't. No clues, no messages, no explanation. No forgiveness. No meaning.

It was stupid of me to think there would be, as usual it was stupid of me to hope. But this time I don't feel angry like I usually do, nor disgusted at my own naiveté. Everything feels empty, but not empty and heavy as it has done for so long, yet light in some way.

I take off my headphones, I have been sitting here for a long time, almost ninety minutes. I have allowed my fingers to slide over an uneven patch on the floor, stared at the wallpaper's floral pattern, as I did so often when I lived here.

Outside the window it has already begun to grow light, the sky is a delicate shade of pink behind the blind. In a few hours it will be morning, it is going to be another lovely day. In a few hours my son will wake, and everything will continue.

ABOUT THE AUTHOR

Therese Bohman grew up outside of Norrköping and now lives in Stockholm. Her debut novel, *Drowned*, received critical acclaim both in Sweden and internationally, and was selected as an Oprah Winfrey Summer Read. Her second novel, *The Other Woman* (Other Press, 2014), was short-listed for the Nordic Council Prize and Swedish Radio's Fiction Prize, while her third novel, *Eventide* (Other Press, 2016), was short-listed for Sweden's most prestigious literary award, the August Prize. Her fourth novel, *Andromeda*, was published by Other Press in 2025. Bohman is an arts journalist who regularly contributes to one of Sweden's largest newspapers, *Expressen*.

ABOUT THE TRANSLATOR

Marlaine Delargy studied Swedish and German at the University of Wales, Aberystwyth, and she taught German for almost twenty years. She has translated novels by many authors, including Kristina Ohlsson; Helene Tursten; John Ajvide Lindqvist; Theodor Kallifatides; Johan Theorin, with whom she won the Crime Writers' Association International Dagger in 2010; and Henning Mankell, with whom she won the Crime Writers' Association International Dagger in 2018. Delargy has also translated nine books in Viveca Sten's Sandhamn Murders series and two books in her Åre Murders series.